Always the Guns

Matt James

A Black Horse Western

ROBERT HALE · LONDON

ISBN 978-0-7090-8820-2

Robert Hale Limited
Clerkenwell House
Clerkenwell Green
London EC1R 0HT

www.halebooks.com

Typeset by
Derek Doyle & Associates, Shaw Heath
Printed and bound in Great Britain by
CPI Antony Rowe, Chippenham and Eastbourne

ONE

ALL THE BRAVE HUNTERS

They knew it was a bear long before they caught the scent or heard the first scuffling sounds coming from the honey stumps.

To young mountain men like them, there was something about a grizzly that charged the air, electrifying, like no other excitement they could name. All along the timbered slopes and ridges of the rugged Bucksaws they knew that others would be hearing it also.

'That a big one you figure, Darry?' whispered Slim Carroway.

'Reckon so,' replied Darien Pell.

5

Shadows had just begun creeping down Big John Hill and there was a fine resiny smell in the air from the pine up on the ridge. The two young friends, Darien Pell and Slim Carroway, were seated atop the tank-stand. Darien's mother was up at the house, soap-boiling. She made soap three times each summer and was hard at work on her second batch today. And it was midsummer in the Misty Mountains of Kentucky. . . .

Darien's sister, five-year-old Phoebe, sat bare-footed with her chubby legs dangling over the porch and singing. Bright-eyed and pretty, she didn't understand there was a bear about or that it was her brother's job to pin-point the animal's position then scent him out with the dogs.

There were five dogs on hand that day: Fang, Roonie, Gawp, Ring and Emerald. They were lying still obediently in the grass nearby, five nondescript mountain hounds each with its eyes focused upon Darien, waiting in quivering expectation for his signal to send them rushing off to run their rib-fat off chasing a bear.

The young men were still trying to identify where the sounds were coming from when Darien's mother appeared in the cabin doorway, wiping her hands on her hessian apron and staring straight up-slope in the direction of Big John Hill. Across at the tank-stand, Darien nudged his friend then indicated his mother.

6

'She always knows when there's bear about,' he whispered. 'That soap in there stinks to high heaven, but she still smells him, I can tell.'

'Hogwash!' muttered Slim. 'She's just come out to get away from that there soap in there.'

They fell silent and gazed out upon the motionless woman for the better part of a minute before she turned towards them sharply.

'There's a bear up along Big John, Darry!'

Darien slammed his friend so hard on the back he lost his balance on the tank-stand. 'What'd I tell you, Slim boy – my mom knows her bears!'

In an instant he was running for the house, a lithe-moving young man, laughing with excitement. 'Hey, Ma, it might be that critter I sighted on Smoky Point last week. Better toss me out my rifle!'

The woman vanished and reappeared moments later toting a Winchester repeater. It was polished and gleamed with store-oil. She checked the weapon expertly then tossed it to her son.

'Don't know that thing'll be all that good agin' a full-growed bear,' she cautioned.

'It's a fine weapon, Ma,' he grinned, working the action and checking the loads. 'Jim Biggles reckons it will kill a bear at two hundred yards.'

'Well, it had better,' she sniffed. 'I've been all out of good bear oil for two months now. It makes for the finest salad dressing in the world, so see you do your best, Darry boy. You've been the best shot in the mountains ever since your pa died and it's time you brought home something to show for it.'

'Sure will, Ma,' he replied, but the woman was already gone – back to her soap making. He turned to Slim. 'You best go get your rifle too.'

Slim slapped the butt of the six-shooter he wore in a holster on his hip. 'No, sir. I'm itching to try this piece against something big.'

'A Colt's not worth beans on big game.'

'You haven't seen me use it of late,' Slim replied, striking a stance with right hand poised over gunbutt. He was tall and lean with a wild thatch of yellow hair. He indicated a blue-stump at the edge of the house clearing. 'Just watch old One-Shot Carroway drill that yonder.'

'Don't go shooting. You'll run the bear!'

'Huh? Oh, all right. But just let me show you how slick I've got on the draw, Darry. It's really something.'

Darien watched patiently as he drew and replaced the Colt in the holster several times. The action was smooth and fast, yet he knew instinctively that he was naturally much quicker on the draw himself, yet virtually never touched a six-gun. Slim would never be better than average with a handgun, but up here in the high country that wasn't important enough to be a handicap.

8

Mostly all they shot up here were raccoons, foxes and the occasional big critter, such as the rare bear. They did it all with rifles.

'Not bad, pard,' he said, poker-faced. 'Providing the critter doesn't get you in its sights first.'

Slim snorted in protest and they wrangled and skylarked around the now gloomy yard, waiting for the moonrise and good bear-hunting time. A pungent scent of soap wafted up from the house and Phoebe emerged and sat on the darkened stoop watching her brother and his friend.

Down below on the path could be heard the crackle of brush and the occasional plopping of berries dropping off trees, these familiar sounds now mingling with distant voices.

Soon they could hear the huntsmen coming. The Pell cabin was the highest dwelling up Big John and it was traditional to start any bear hunt from up there in the piney woods.

Snipe Evans and his sons arrived first: Ethan, Esaw and Edgaston. They had seven dogs and Old Snipe toted his six-foot long flintlock rifle. Next came Ruby O'Mara and the Jessup boys and Grandpa Alden and his grandson Petey.

Pretty soon there were near twenty men standing in the house yard, most of them inveterate huntsmen who'd talked about little other than bear all week. At the moment they were all but totally quiet, waiting for Grandpa Alden to lead them out. He'd led every bear hunt for fifty years, from the days back when the Misty Mountains were full of Indians and more grizzlies than a man could count.

Grandpa Alden shut his eyes and stood with head tilted back in a listening attitude. After what seemed quite a time his eyes snapped wide and he shouted, 'I can tell that bear's on Red Ridge in the honey stumps. Reckon it's gotta be the same one my grandboy Petey sighted across by Top Peak yesterday.'

'Big one, Petey?' Darien wanted to know.

'Surely was, Darrie,' the youth responded eagerly. 'Mebbe the biggest I ever did see.'

'I calculated he was sizable by the tracks.' Darien paused as from higher up came the short, deep cough of a big animal with its snout clogged up with honey. He slapped his hip and shouted, 'Let's get going!'

The huntsmen parted to allow Grandpa Alden to lead them off, then closed ranks and followed. There were three times as many hounds as hunters. This was as it should be and all the dogs were on leads. Time enough to set them loose when they reached Red Ridge.

Despite his years, Gramps made good time up the steep climb. 'Bear huntin' pleasures me more'n most anythin' I know,' he had been saying for half a century, and had the scars to prove that he'd not always come off victorious in such ventures.

Up out of the pines in the moonlight climbed a brute of a moon as big as they ever got anywhere in Missouri, a huntsman's moon. The dogs strained at their leashes all the way up to the rim of the gully where Grandpa Alden held up his hand to bring the party to a halt.

All listened. There was no sound from farther up at first, and all they could see were the black pockets of gulleys and hollows where the springs ran cold even in midsummer.

Behind the old man, Evans's blue hound whined sharply before Esaw gripped its muzzle and cut off the sounds. The moment there was full silence all heard the grunting coming from the darkest and deepest section of the ridge. Grandpa swung his arm over in a sweeping gesture and they went after him, quiet and gun-ready now as they worked their way around the limestone tooth.

Darien and Slim traded excited grins and Slim humped his back and spread his arms wide in a passable imitation of a rampaging bear. Behind, sober Luke Jessup grunted disapprovingly so Slim quit fooling up and hurried on.

Next time the old man halted they sensed their quarry was close. None of the hounds whined now but you could feel the eagerness brimming out of them with that biting bear-scent pungent on the wild night air.

'Darry!' Grandpa hissed. 'You handle a rifle tolerable well and can move about quiet enough. Get yourself up to Hanrohan's Still. If the critter gets too riled up he'll likely highball past there so's to get the piney woods all around himself again.'

Alden frowned suspiciously at Slim Carroway when he came up to stand alongside Darien, looking confident. The leader was in charge of all parts of the hunt and nobody was permitted to question his authority – just do whatever he said. But plainly, Slim wanted to go up to Hanrohan's Still. Grandpa, rubbing his flat belly and chomping on his chaw tobacco, saw this and relented. 'All right, boy, off you go. But for pity's sake don't start up your eternal gabbin'.'

Slim shot away without even taking offence at the warning. He could still see Darien who was moving stealthily across the bunch-grass cutback that skirted Red Ridge.

Over the ridge and high up along Big John, there was a faint glimmer-shine of moonlight on a metal roof. Along with producing the best corn liquor in fifty miles, Hanrohan's Still provided the best look-out spot in the mountain. Perched high on its tin flank, a man could stand and cover a vast sweep of terrain from an excellent shooting position should game happen to show.

The two were still within sight of the main group lower down when Edgaston Evans's dog shucked its leash.

It shot like an arrow through the pack, slithering and skittering in its excitement, head down and tail up, a hunting dog in full joyous flight.

The animal made no sound until well clear of the hunters and then let out its hunting howl. It was the kind of wild, spine-tingling sound that raised goose bumps on the skin of strong men and caused the hounds to tug and yelp in their frenzy to be free.

Old Alden gave his familiar piercing yell that had been ringing around the Misties for decades and the whole hillside seemed to burst into uproar. Shouts, howling hounds and the scrabbling of boots on rocks filled the night, before there came a kind of explosion from the blackness of the deepest thickets and the bear loomed in full sight against the moon.

The animal's sheer size seemed to confuse them all momentarily, its higher position and the way it was silhouetted making it to appear ten feet tall.

The loose hound bounded over the crest and charged in to attack with a yelp of pure joy.

There was a blur of movement, a chopped-off howl of pain, and the dog was tumbling brokenly back down the slope. When they looked up the bear was gone.

Darien alone got off a shot but knew he'd been far too slow and high.

It was moments before Luke Jessup finally broke the awed silence.

'He's a monster!'

'He killed Gentle!' Evans raged, standing over his broken blue hound.

'This ain't a-boilin' beans,' Grandpa Allen trumpeted, already scrabbling up the ridge slope. 'C'mon, we got us a bear to get!'

The party quickly spread out across the face of Big John. The moon climbed higher, not quite the size it had been earlier yet almost as bright as midday now. The bear was working itself higher in the direction of the still, moving fast. The younger men, Darien and Slim, along with the Evans boys and Petey Alden were right on the heels of the hounds. All the dogs had been set loose by this, their tumultuous chorus ringing from one gully-point to another.

Quickly drawing ahead of the rest, Darien and Slim drew up beneath a black fir tree to fight for breath after clambering two hundred yards almost straight up.

'It's still . . . travellin' fast,' Slim gasped, sucking in great lungfuls of air.

From above and over to the west of the crest, the

14

voices of the hounds rang out excitingly in the night.

'Never catch him this way,' gasped Darien. 'But I figure he's pushing west towards the valley. If we cut down over Morgan's Hill we might just get to cut him off down below. Wouldn't be surprised if he's got a notion to swim across the river.' He slapped the stock of his new rifle. 'He'll play hell with the dogs if he suckers them into the water, so let's make time!'

Slim rarely questioned the other's judgment and rushed off in his wake. He had holstered the Colt again, now needed all his agility and balance to keep from falling in the black-shadowed holes and slides along Red Ridge.

Charging past moon-washed rocks and down steepled corridors of pines the two went, aware of the dimishing sounds of the hunt now. Half a mile down, Darien abruptly halted and glanced upwards. 'Listen. He's heading straight up by the still,' he said disappointedly. He sighed gustily and leaned a hand on the tree trunk. 'No point busting ourselves now – he's game for somebody else's gun up there.'

Slim stood bent over in the clearing, slapping his sides. 'Whew! Reckon they must be right when they say tobacco cuts your wind.'

'You only chaw about once a week. Anyway, what's that got to do with the bear?'

'Let's face it – the bear is finished for us. You brought us the wrong way off the hill.'

'I notice you followed me fast enough.'

'Only 'cause you get ornery if anybody tells you you're wrong.'

The argument heated up swiftly, vigorous and familiar from a lifetime of friendship. Finally they broke off and simply stood staring silently across the blue-moon mountains to the distant valley where both lived.

'Daffy?'

'Huh?' he replied, half-listening to Slim and half-focusing on the sounds of the distant bear hunt.

'When are we goin' to head West?'

Darien gusted out a lungful of air. Going west was something they'd talked and dreamed about for years. A romantic dream in their school days, a fading thing in the busy years of growing up, yet sharper and keener now than ever before during this, his twenty-first year.

Most men married early in the Misty Mountains. Married, settled, reproduced and worked hard. Mostly, that was. But the pards were aware they'd always felt differently, that they were of a different stamp than the rest of Bucksaw youth – Slim bursting with furious energy and with a giant thirst for life, Darien, strong and capable beyond his years and unwilling to bury

16

himself in the hill country here while men younger than themselves were carving glory and success for themselves in that great unknown world west of the Mississippi.

And Darien wondered if this could be just another 'Let's do it – but not quite yet' moment such as they'd shared many a time before. Or maybe, just maybe, it might prove to be *The Moment* – the day and the hour they would actually look one another in the eye and decide that – if ever a giant step had to be taken then it must be *now*.

'Why . . . why not now?' he heard himself say in what sounded almost like a stranger's voice.

Slim straightened sharply. 'You on the level or just talking to hear yourself?'

That was a big question yet Darien was amazed how quickly and easily he answered it – as if it had all been decided in a single moment in his mind.

'I reckon Ma will be pretty lonesome when I'm gone, her being a widow and all. Phoebe too . . . and she's just a squirt. . . .'

'You're really serious then?'

'Why, I surely do reckon I am,' he replied, his voice growing stronger. 'I mean, we've been promising for years we'd go, and who's to say we'd ever find a better time to do it than right now while—'

His words were engulfed as gunfire erupted and

washed down from above. They sprang to their feet to hear the ongoing shooting punctuated by the howling of hounds and the hoarse cries of huntsmen.

'They've nailed him!' Slim breathed.

'Not sure,' Darien countered.

'What do you mean?'

'That was shotgun fire we just heard.'

'But none of our party's toting shotguns today.'

'Dead right.' A pause, then, 'But Hanrohan and his boys sure have them. Their "revenuer" guns, they call them.'

'They must've nailed the big critter when he was trying to get back to the piney woods in back.'

'Could be. But I doubt they'd bag this one. Those boys are no marksmen, what with old Hanrohan always sampling the corn liquor and the boys not much better.'

They stood in tense silence for another minute before Darien suddenly tensed, turning away from the hill slopes with head cocked sharply, listening hard. Taut seconds slipped by before he suddenly swung back to the other with a broad smile. 'That critter is coming down Morgan's and making for the river by Foxglove Draw!'

'Well, hell! Let's go!'

They flew down the steep slope, at times barely seeming to touch ground. They were in the grip of bear fever and even while running pell-mell could

18

smell him stronger and stronger with every stride, heard his crashing downhill progress.

They made the river well ahead of their quarry and could still hear it making its noisy descent as they stood with chests heaving and excitement flushing their faces.

'He's going to hit the creek higher up,' Slim predicted.

'You're right. And when he gets there, we'll be there waiting. C'mon!'

But Slim suddenly reached out and seized Darien's shirtsleeve. 'But that'd take us on to Wiggs's land, pard.'

Darien halted, frowned, cursed. 'Damn, so it will!'

'You know how old Hogue Wiggs don't allow nobody to trespass on his dirt, more especially so ever since he got elected to mayor and decided that raised him about a dozen notches higher than everybody else in the county. And then, you and Corey ain't that friendly neither.'

'Damnit!' Darien panted. For what the other said was only too true. Rich and powerful Mayor Wiggs was a huge landowner and power broker with no time for folks from higher up along the slopes of Big John – 'crackers' as he called them. His son Corey was a replica of the old man but lacked ruthlessness, that quality which dominated Hogue senior's whole character. Darien and young

19

Wiggs both called on Betty Lou Berne from the far side of Big John. Corey and Darien had even come to blows over her last summer with Wiggs soundly defeated. The two had been feuding ever since – mountain style.

Darry cocked his head, listening.

No doubt about it; that critter sounded as if it was making directly across the Wiggs's bottom lands in order to get to the river. The temptation to jump the dividing fence and go on to head across was strong – particularly when it involved quarry as exciting and challenging as the biggest bear sighted around Bucksaw over a long hot summer. Nonetheless, he sighed and shook his head.

'Too chancy, boy. Not worth the risk.'

Slim cursed and squinted up at the tall black trees silhouetted against and silvery moonlight of the Wiggs's lowlands acres. The headquarters lay out of sight a good mile from the river where they were standing. Maybe it could be possible for them to nail that critter then haul it off enemy land without tangling with Wiggs . . . couldn't it?

'What the hell!' he burst out suddenly. 'We don't mean to harm nothing but that critter, Darrie. Surely a free man's got the right to hunt a bear wherever he runs?'

Darien grappled with temptation. Bear-hunting was in their blood. Nothing excited like hunting a big, bad bear. Yet still he shook his head. 'Nope, we've just got to set back and let him run free, damnit!'

'But, hell burn it—'

'That's final. I don't want any more ruckusing with Wiggs.'

Whenever Darien spoke in that tone of voice, with eyebrows drawn down tight over his eyes, his pard knew there was no point in wrangling. So Slim just dropped a muttered a curse and fell silent.

All was still. . . .

Without warning the bear exploded out of the timberline on all fours, a huge mass of blackness streaking across a wide piece of open ground as though all the hounds of hell were at his heels, rocketing downslope and ripping up turf with outsized paws.

Suddenly the bear lurched to a stop in mid-stride, scenting them but not sighting them yet.

It rose up on its hind legs in the moonlight like Moses proclaiming the Laws.

Then it was down again, big, black and devil-quick, racing for the water. Approaching the fence by Foxglove Draw like a freight train, it launched its massive body into the air and cleared the top rail by three feet, hit the ground running and set off for the timbers beyond Wiggs's corn acres.

A shot rang out.

21

The bear faltered and changed directions, now coming at a tangent towards the two men. Darien was scanning for sight of the shooter when Slim clapped his shoulder.

'Look yonder! It's Corey Wiggs!'

In moments the rider rode into full view mounted on one of his father's saddle-horses. He had a smoking rifle in hand and was yelling excitedly. But the bear was still well ahead of the rider and every giant stride brought it closer to the dividing fence where Darien and Slim were standing, guns up, yet uncertain.

'Don't you varmints durst shoot!' they heard the horseman bawl across the night. 'He's on Wiggs land and that makes him rightful Wiggs property!'

'A man ought to cut loose – just to see what that horse's ass would do about it,' Slim growled. Then he cursed when the horseman shouldered his rifle again. 'That fool can't expect to hit nothing shooting off of horseback thataway and—'

The rest of his words were drowned out by the booming voice of the Winchester. The slug whined off rocks close by the bear, causing the critter to veer sharply. Now it was coming directly towards the two where they stood on the lower side of the boundary fence.

Slim whipped out his Colt but Darien seized his arm.

'Don't shoot – use your head!' he yelled. 'I don't

22

reckon he's sighted us yet. If we don't scare him off he's liable to come clear over the fence, the way he's running. If he does that then he'll be ours to bring down – legal!'

Meantime Corey Wiggs, although a dab hand with a rifle, was setting himself a formidable task. Shooting from well behind a fast-moving bear from the back of a horse galloping full tilt over uneven ground through moonlight shadows, made uncertain conditions even for a star marksman.

His next shot missed its target by yards but the roar of the weapon spurred the critter to even greater speed – and now the dividing fence loomed close.

'Don't you durst, you crackers!' Wiggs roared. 'He's mine, damn you!'

Slim made to retort but Darien silenced him. Both crouched lower as the grizzly bounded knee-deep through the rough damp growth, drawing close to the fence now. They could hear its deep body-grunting and its wild scent came even stronger.

Slim panted, 'He's ours for sure now, Darry. We'll let him have it as he goes over!'

Darien readied for the shot of his life. As the beast bunched itself up before launching its great bulk into a leap, to be momentarily silhouetted huge and dark against the moonlit sky for just a moment, he squinted along the blued-steel barrel and squeezed the trigger.

At first it seemed he'd missed as the critter landed on their side of the fence on all fours and continued to run.

Then the rifle thundered again and the animal crashed down headlong with one mammoth hiss of escaping breath, rolled twice and never moved again.

Corey Riggs was white-faced and livid as he tight-reined his mount to a sliding halt the other side of the fence. 'That varmint is mine!' he shouted.

'I don't see your brand on him, Wiggs,' Slim Carroway jeered excitedly.

'He was on our land. On *Wiggs* land!'

'Don't go getting yourself into a ringtail, Corey,' Darien said calmly enough even though well aware of the potential danger in the situation. 'He's dead on our side of the fence, brought down by our guns so there's no way you can claim him. You had your chance and you botched it. Game's over.'

'He was mine!' Corey repeated shrilly, and they both became aware that he was even drunker than they'd realised. He glared balefully at Darien for a long moment before shuddering and drawing in a ragged breath. 'Seems like you aim to grab *everything* that belongs to me, Pell!' he mouthed venomously.

'What do you mean by that?'

24

'Betty Lou's what I mean, like you know.'

Darien stiffened. 'I whupped you for bandying her name about before, Corey. You looking for more of the same?'

'I called on her just this evenin',' Wiggs grated. 'I knew you wouldn't be seein' her . . . not with a bear about, you wouldn't. I told her that, too,' he added with malice. He was a well-built man of Darien's age, broad of shoulder and handsome in an arrogant way.

'Big of you,' Darien retorted, holding on to his anger. 'What else did you tell her?'

'I told her I mean to marry her.'

'Guess you might say you said too damned much then.'

'She threw me out!' the man raged, swaying in the saddle. 'You hear that, Pell? Me, a Wiggs, gettin' thrown out of any poor cracker's place! And worse, she told me she's in love with you. I told her she was loco and that she was welcome to you – good and welcome!'

'Still talking too much . . . I'd move on if I was you, Wiggs.'

'Yeah, go buy some votes for your daddy,' Slim jeered.

Rage suffused Wiggs's face. He made to bring up the Winchester but Darien's six-gun leapt to cover him.

'Don't be an idiot, Corey!' he said. 'There'll be

no gunplay here . . . no need for it.'

It seemed a long tense moment before the rifle slowly lowered to angle at the ground. Darien let his own weapon angle down with a sigh of relief.

'Best go to home and sleep it off, Corey,' he said in a neutral tone.

Wiggs appeared too angry and frustrated to retort. His face still distorted, he swung his horse about. Darien and Slim traded wordless glances when some impulse caused Darien to cut his attention back to Wiggs again.

The man wasn't riding off now but appeared to be sneaking something from beneath his left shoulder. Moonlight glinted on derringer steel with a snarling face above it. The weapon reached firing level to spew gunflame with the bullet whipping so close that Darien felt the hot airwhip of its passage.

Instinct saw him jerk his rifle back into the firing position. He shouted a warning to the man with the gun but it went unheeded. Wiggs's smoking weapon held two chambers, and he was aiming for a second shot when Darien fired. Wiggs vanished momentarily in a cloud of powder-smoke and as it cleared he was revealed sitting stock-still in his saddle staring at Darien as though in disbelief. Then he tumbled from the saddle to crash face down across the dividing fence.

Slim was first to reach Corey Wiggs. He turned

him over to see his face then drew back, his face drained of all color. 'Glory be, the man's dead, Darry. Shot plumb through the heart!'

TWO

RUN OUT FROM BUCKSAW

'Darry . . . Darry?'

Her voice reached him through the midnight quiet, like music. It hurt to hear her calling like that. She sounded child-like and fearful – and he knew he was the cause of that.

He stepped clear of the rocks that had concealed him. 'Here I am, Betty Lou.'

She rushed to him and for a long minute he simply held her tight. He could feel her heart pounding. Everything he'd ever felt for Betty Lou welled up in him now they were parting. He gazed over her head at the trace of the winding wagon trail which led from Oakley Berne's place then up and around the flank of Big John Hill and finally on to Bucksaw. As soon as Slim appeared down that road he would have to go – maybe forever. He hoped Slim would get here ahead of the posse that would surely appear any moment – a posse with Hogue Wiggs doubtless riding at its head.

He'd already heard that Wiggs had announced he would settle for nothing less than a life for a life in retaliation for the 'murder' of his only son. In another man that might simply be regarded as grief talking. But with Hogue Wiggs you knew he meant every word.

'You're cold, Darry,' Betty Lou said, holding him at arm's length and studying him with huge eyes. 'Real cold.'

'No ... no I'm not.' He realized he was trembling, forced a reassuring smile. 'What are you doing up here anyway?'

'There's a hot meal for you down to the house. I fried you some pork chops and side meat with hominy grits and ... and some black-eyed peas, just as you like them. I also made a poke of vittles for you to take and ... and ... oh, Darry, Darry!'

She clung to him again and sobbed as though she could not stop. He murmured reassuring words against her hair yet she was inconsolable. Only the eventual appearance of her father in the lighted doorway of the family home below finally saw her break apart and struggle to bring her emotions into check.

'Chow's a-gettin' cold, Darry boy!' the broad Missouri voice called up to where they stood upon the look-out rocks.

'Coming, Oakley!' he replied. He held Betty Lou at arm's length and dabbed her tears with his kerchief. Somehow she managed a smile, even if it was wan and pallid.

'I shouldn't be like this,' she said. 'I promised I would be brave – but I just can't help it. I'm a coward, I suppose. You'll be better off without me, Darry – wherever you're going.'

'Don't ever say that,' he chided. 'Not ever! Come on, come down with me and we can grab a little more time while I eat.'

'No. Pa said I'm to stay up here while you're at supper, and keep a lookout for Slim – or for the Wiggs men. But, darling, why does it have to be this way? Surely there's no need to run like an outlaw. Corey tried to kill you – no court could find you anything but innocent of murder under those circumstances.'

'I explained before, honey,' he said quietly, only fully realizing the true scope of the disaster himself now. 'Hogue Wiggs is mayor of Bucksaw and the most powerful man in a hundred miles. And Corey was his only son. So, he'd never rest until he had me swinging from a tree, and he's got

30

enough power and influence to succeed in doing just that.'

'But where will you go? What will you do?'

'Don't rightly know as yet, Betty Lou. . . .'

He looked away, lean face tight and grim. He was a fugitive now, was beginning to think and act like one. He'd been driven to save his own life with a gun, yet had realized the very moment Corey Wiggs tumbled dead from his saddle that Hogue Wiggs would never quit until his son was avenged.

He still didn't know what he would do or where he might go.

It was all he could do to grapple with the notion of life as a fugitive without planning what he might do once clear of the Misty Mountains.

Oakley Berne shouted up to them again. Darien kissed the girl hastily and hurried down the slope to the house.

Betty Lou's father sat opposite him while he ate. Yet he had little appetite, even though the food was delicious and he was aware he would need good vittles inside if he wanted to outrun a Wiggs posse.

'Where's Slim aimin' to find a hoss for you, Darry?' Berne wanted to know. He was a big-boned share-cropper with eyes as clear as a child's and a heart as big as Kentucky.

'Don't rightly know, Oakley. But you know Slim.

He'll come up with something for me to ride, even if it's only a jackass.'

'Only wished I had some better horse-flesh to offer, son. You'd be more than welcome. But only folks like Hogue Wiggs get to run fancy bloodstock in this county.'

Darien kept eating and made no comment, his thoughts grappling with whatever future was awaiting a young man who'd never ventured farther than fifty miles of where he'd been born. Until now.

The older man leaned back in his chair with a growl.

'It's all wrong . . . you boys having to run like criminals just for protecting yourselves. But I still know you're doing the right thing . . . the only thing. And at the risk of repeating myself, never forget that rich bastard is the most vindictive man in this territory with more power and influence than anybody has a right to. So when you go, make certain you go far and fast and leave no sign. Hear?'

Darien nodded and the other man sighed.

'Well, this county voted Wiggs in as mayor recent and soon enough they'll be findin' out just what breed of polecat they've saddled themselves with. Only wish I'd known before about that Corey comin' over here moonin' over Betty Lou. Maybe I'd have plugged him myself if

I could've foreseen what was goin' to happen 'twixt you and him. You're scarce full-growed yet but Hogue Wiggs won't hesitate to stand you on a gibbet this year, next year – if it takes him forever. That's the kind of hater he is. But it just ain't right that he can manipulate the law and fit a murder charge on one of the the finest young fellers in the hills.'

Darien had quit eating, moved by the other's loyalty and affection. He was realizing just how painful it would be to leave all these people and maybe never get to see any of their faces again. He gazed around the kitchen, memorizing everything in order he might recall it as it was when he was long gone from this good place – somewhere.

'Finish up them hog-chops,' he was ordered. 'No man can ride on an empty belly.'

'I've had my fill,' he said, rising. He crossed the room with a lithe stride and took his Winchester down from the wall. 'I'd best pack up then let Betty Lou come back on down.'

'Here's your sack, boy,' Oakley said, hefting a leather saddle-bag. He grinned. 'Tucked a few dollars I took from what I was savin' towards my next big blowout in Bucksaw. It'll do you far more good than it would me.'

Darien paused in the doorway reflecting on the care and loyalty of all the good folks in the county. He straightened sharply as Betty Lou's cry carried down from upslope.

'Horse coming . . . only the one . . . I think!'

Darien gripped the older man's hand and squeezed hard, then was quickly gone out into the night beneath a massive moon. As he climbed the slope he cocked an ear to drumming sounds drifting down faintly from beyond the crest. He stiffened upon realizing that two horses were approaching at a hard run.

Friends or foes?

He was expecting Slim yet it could be anybody. He stopped as Betty Lou suddenly emerged from the gloom to seize his arm, panting breathlessly.

'Two horses coming in, Darry. I couldn't see if it was Slim for certain but I'm near certain one saddle is empty.'

'Then that has to be Slim,' he replied with more assurance than he felt. He knew if it proved to be Wiggs riders he was prepared to gun them down to the last man or else go down shooting himself.

He'd traveled that far in a few brief hours; had changed that much.

The sudden stutter of nearing hoofbeats crossing the hard gravel of the road by the hog pens came clearly. He raised and cocked the Winchester, feeling almost like a desperado.

Moments later Slim Carroway burst into full view astride one fine-looking mount and leading another to clatter into the yard and then dusted to a halt before him. Darien snatched the lines of the free animal then looked up, wide-eyed and astonished.

'Tell me I'm not seeing right,' he half-grinned. 'These look exactly like two of those blood horses Wiggs had shipped in from Savannah recent!'

'Dead on target, *amigo*,' Carroway chuckled. 'I figured that seein' as how he's forcin' us to run like crooks Wiggs should at least be responsible for us traveling proper mounted. I lifted this pair from his top forty half an hour ago. It was like takin' candy offen a kid!'

'*Us*, you just said. What do you mean – us? I'm running . . . it's me they want to hang.'

'I'm going with you. Now, don't start wrangling. I've got no kin to hold me here, like you know. And seeing as I was with you when Corey cashed in I reckon Wiggs would do his damndest to see that I swung alongside you – so here I am.'

'Look, this isn't any game. When I quit this county I'll be an outlaw. You got any notion what that can mean?'

'Sure I do. But like I say, it'd be far riskier for me around Bucksaw with you gone.'

Carroway's trademark grin flashed as he hipped around in the saddle to study what could be seen of the trail, plainly excited by it all. Yet he was sober when he turned back.

'Guess you should knew I sighted Wiggs leading

a whole passel of riders down past the falls just half an hour back. They were riding like fools – I could hear that son-of-a-bitch urging them on.'

A taut moment's silence. Then, 'How many in the bunch?' Darien panted as he thonged the food-sack to a saddle-clip.

'Ten . . . twelve mebbe.'

Darien went momentarily still. But he recovered quickly to complete the chore. 'You know, I didn't calculate there'd be that many fellers in all Bucksaw ready to take Hogue Wiggs's word against mine . . . much less saddle up and ride with him.'

'Well, you wouldn't be so surprised if you got a look at them.' Slim paused to spit contemptuously. 'Jokers like Tooner and Brougham, along with Stinker O'Malley's coon-catchers from over Maple Creek way. Of course there's a couple you'd expect better from, like Ed Gunkel and Leander Craig. . . .'

His voice trailed away, then came back strongly. 'But this is no time to jaw. It might be a mongrel pack Wiggs has put together, but they'll do whatever he pays them to do and if they nab us I don't have to tell you we'd be lynched. Wiggs would have to handle things that way on account he'd know he could never rig a murder conviction against you in any court.'

'Did you get to see Ma?'

'No. Wiggs has got your place staked out by the Donovan boys and John Edgar. No chance of sneaking by those scum.'

Darien turned to the girl at his side. 'Betty Lou, will you see Ma and say goodbye for me? No time to get back there now . . . and they'd be waitin' for me anyhow.'

'Of course, Darry. I'll tell her you'll hole up at Moose Canyon until the posse disappears and that you plan to cross the river into the west, riding until things calm down. She'll believe that lie . . . for a time, at least. I don't think she realizes just how far you might be forced to run . . . or if you'll ever come back. . . .'

'Nor do I. But I'll write and send money soon as I can. And tell Phoebe to mind her manners and—'

'Cut it, damnit, Darry!' Slim cut in urgently. 'Betty Lou, get him moving, will you?'

'He's right, Darry – oh, listen! I can hear horses now!'

They stood in silence until they picked up the faint yet distinct beat of hoofs upon the trail – many hoofs.

Darien hipped around in the saddle for one last glimpse at the girl he loved. Their eyes met and locked before Carroway's urgent voice broke the spell. 'Hurry, man – shift them stumps!'

'Coming – damnit!'

With a curse, Darien wheeled his mount about in its own length, and now everything he treasured in life lay behind him.

'We'll go over the Razorback by Dintana Creek!' he shouted. And touched steel to horsehide.

The horse broke into a run and Slim came drumming close behind. They stormed from the yard, dipped from sight a moment beyond the barns and then Betty Lou and Oakley could see them climbing the bluegrass rise a quarter-mile distant, which would take them all the way up to the Razorback – and beyond.

The watchers listened to the hoofbeats swiftly fade, soon to be replaced by the sounds of the oncoming posse. Moments later the fleeing riders dropped from sight and were gone.

A cool breeze rose just at that moment, fingering the tips of the pines by the barn and rattling the loose chip-tiles upon the washhouse roof. A fine cloud of hoof-lifted dust drifted lazily overhead as Oakley joined his daughter and placed an arm about her shoulders.

'Will he ever come back, Pa?' Her voice sounded surprisingly calm and strong.

'Sure he will, honey. Darien Pell has got steel behind that easy-going way of his. He's been throwed by all that's happened, sure, but his kind was born to buck the odds. Yeah, you'll see him back setting on this here stoop soon enough, you take it from your old dad.'

'And I'll wait for him . . . forever if I must. . . .'

They had their first real taste of what leaving could be like when they stopped to spell their mounts in the thin high air atop the Razorback. This rocky spine of the high country was the unofficial western boundary of Kell County, and as soon as you dipped down the western flank the Misty Mountains would be lost from sight.

Slim had never been beyond Razorback before while Darien had been as far as Hymas City some twenty miles west. Yet this moment was just as significant for him as it was to his pard – the dividing line between the old life and the new.

Both felt very young and melancholy standing there beside their blowing horses and staring back.

Eventually Darien forced a grin and adjusted his hat. 'Better keep going, Slim. Plenty rough miles between here and Moose Canyon.'

They were up and off within moments. A mile farther on, Darien led the way off the trail and ducked beneath the drooping arms of a great piñon tree. Crossing the meadow beyond they forded a yellow stream filled with frogs and followed it downland, passing from gnarled old cottonwoods that cast blue-black moonshadows over pink river sand to reach a point where a vast and sleeping lilac field spread out directly beyond.

'How much farther to this Moose Canyon now?' Slim asked some time later.

'Around ten miles.'

'What if they trail us there?'

'Don't fret, we'll still lose them.'

A trailing creeper slashed at his face as he turned to the trail before him. Huge ashes and elms loomed up between limestone sentinels and black soil strips with towering rising walls of ash-gray rock showing beyond.

It seemed a long slow time before they finally left the heavy timber behind to sight the pale-yellow walls of Moose Canyon looming eerily before them.

'If anyone's dogging us we'll lose them over the next five miles,' Darien called back confidently, banging heels against horse-hide.

'How can you be sure?'

'I came here hunting once. Beyond that pinnacle yonder there's old animal trails spraying out in all directions, mostly over stone and rock of some kind. You can ride to and fro across that landscape all day without leaving a sign even a Cherokee tracker could read, if you pick your trail. Yessir, we're heading West and in two days we'll be in the next territory where nobody can touch us.'

'Two days?' Slim's voice sounded exhausted.

'Standing on our heads. C'mon, stow the jawbone and keep riding.'

*

Hogue Wiggs coughed into his kerchief but didn't shift his gaze from the trail ahead.

'Break up into bunches of five and cover both sides of the river, the north pass and then the road all the way to the stage trail,' he barked in a voice that was accustomed to be listened to and obeyed. 'And five of you stay with me.'

There was a clatter of hoofs and rising dust which slowly drifted away as five men sat their saddles waiting for the sixth to speak again.

'We'll stop off at Willigan's Crossings,' Wiggs announced in a voice growing stronger now the coughing attack had passed. He inhaled deeply, his powerful face a taut-skinned mask in the moonlight. 'Any man with messages to leave can do so there. Tell your kin we'll be back when my son's murderers are dead and not before.'

Some appeared nervous, others downright scared. Yet none dared raise his voice in protest even though it was now growing plain they would be expected to commit to the hunt for the killers indefinitely.

Wiggs slammed horsehide with boot-heels and they splashed across the low creek then galloped up the rising trail beyond.

Forty-eight hours later found Pell and Carroway older, wiser and infinitely wearier riders-on-the-run as they unsaddled and attended to travel-stained horses. Some time later they hunkered down by a brave little camp fire on the windy flank of a boulder-littered downslope high above a stream of which even Darien did not pretend to know the name.

'Are you sure we ain't lost?' Slim Carroway asked in an exhausted monotone.

'No chance. Here, toss a few more sticks on the fire.'

Carroway didn't move. His eyes were hollow from fatigue and he had the uneasy feeling there wasn't a saloon within one hundred miles.

'You've been bull-dusting me for days,' he accused. ' "Just a few miles farther, pard." Or, "If not the next hill, the one after that will see us in Jingletown" . . . or maybe that should be Starvation City. C'mon, Darry, you know we are lost, so at least be a man and own up to it!'

But Darien just grinned, determined to maintain a brave face and confident manner until certain they were lost. At this point, he only *suspected* he might have taken a wrong turn at the canyon crossing five miles back. Never any point in admitting a mistake until you were dead sure, he reasoned.

By the time he had vittles heated and they were tucking into them with gusto, Carroway appeared more cheerful yet still kept glancing over his shoulder or down along the canyon slopes. For this was a genuinely spooky tract of wild country with gaunt and windblown trees sighing overhead and strange animal cries drifting up from the piney woods across the canyon.

Nonetheless, by the time they were through eating and Darien was hustling about with renewed energy to build up the fire against the chill that would come with the night – no more than an hour ahead now – there was a feeling almost of contentment up there upon that rocky slope with full bellies and a jolt or two of rye whiskey already doing their healing work.

They hunkered down close by the fire and were yarning away almost cheerfully when Darien broke off in mid-sentence to whirl about and stare upslope, hand on Colt butt.

'What?' Carroway said, squinting around and seeing nothing.

'Dunno,' Darien said, rising and massaging the back of his neck with his free hand. He surveyed gaunt rocks and wind-blasted trees suspiciously, squinted at the falling sun then turned about to check on the horses standing hipshot and weary, played-out, nearby.

Nothing, he eventually decided, feeling a little foolish. For he was not by nature given to shying at shadows, had always instinctively felt easy and at home in the wilds.

He had hunkered down once again when it happened. From somewhere close by – surprisingly close – came the voice.

'On your feet and reach!'

Darien instinctively grabbed his Colt handle but did not draw. For in that instant the gaunt, broad-shouldered figure of the man holding a Winchester repeater aimed at his belt buckle emerged like some kind of badlands apparition from a nest of ancient gray rocks less than a hundred feet distant.

For seconds which seemed an eternity long, a frozen Darien realized the rifleman must have snaked his way downhill from the timberline and used the cover of the rocks and deadwood clusters over some fifty yards in order to draw so close.

Either this night-comer was a natural stalker or else he and Slim had done what no men on the run should ever do – let their guard down!

Either way, they were in trouble. One look at the six-footer with the cud of chaw tobacco bulging his cheek and that rifle as steady as a rock in his hands was all it took to know that.

He cursed impotently beneath his breath, as the rifleman said, 'Drop your gunbelts and move away from them. And try and remember – I never miss!'

He was convincing. The pards traded glances, shrugged in resignation, did as ordered.

The moment their gunbelts were taken the rifleman, dressed like a preacher in a dark broadcloth suit, wedged a thumb and forefinger between his teeth to emit a shrill whistle. Instantly upslope in a stand of windblown oaks, movement stirred and quickly took on the shapes of two more figures with guns and rifles emerging from cover to stand motionless staring down at them.

The big preacher man with the big gun halted ten feet away and allowed his rifle to angle towards the ground.

'Just shavetails!' he snorted. 'We figgered you could be . . . well, never mind what.' His hard eyes studied each man in turn but he didn't appear impressed. 'All right, who are you and what the hell are you doing here? If you don't come up with the right answers, you're dead meat!'

'We're just . . . just drifting,' Darien insisted. He jerked a thumb over his shoulder. 'Looking to do a little hunting and maybe some fishing and—'

'And lyin'!' the big man cut him off. 'C'mon, I've been watching you for a couple of miles now. You're on the dodge . . . lookin' backtrail every hundred yards and fiddling with your shooters like you might be expectin' to use 'em.' He paused to draw closer and study them even more intently. 'Look like a couple of rubes to me, but then I

45

could be wrong. What do you say, pards?'

His henchmen, one young and hard-faced, the other sinister but relaxed-looking behind a neat mustache, emerged from brushy cover to look them over. They appeared anything but impressed.

'Bounty hunters can come in all shapes and sizes, you know, Reverend,' remarked the young tough. He turned his head to spit. 'But if that is their real brand then they look about as scary as my Aunt Hetty.'

The mustachioed gunman at his elbow chipped in. 'These here ain't no bounty men, *amigos*,' he insisted. 'Look at their prads and the way they let 'em get all worn down and ragged. Anyways, who'd go huntin' badmen to hell and gone in this shank of the woods anyway?'

'*We're* here, ain't we?' pointed out the first man, plainly the leader. 'Anyway, we don't have time to waste. Give us one good reason for us not to believe you're just a couple of dirty bounty-huntin' dudes who've taken a wrong bend in the trail and are just beggin' to pay for your mistake.'

Darien's throat felt tight. 'Look, fellas—' he began, but the leader with the look of a preacher cut him off.

'Empty your pockets,' he ordered. 'Put your stuff on that boulder yonder. Connie, go check out their gear. C'mon, hustle, we don't have all day!'

They did as ordered under the watchful gaze of

the young outlaw, whose name, they learnt, was Connie Gaillard. The gunmen appeared disappointed not to find anything incriminating.

'I still say they look shifty,' muttered the young one with the gunslinger look. 'So . . . what are they doing to hell and gone out here anyway? That huntin', fishin' buffalo dust don't wash with us nohow, do it, Durling?'

'The man's right,' sighed Durling waving his gun barrel. 'Better come up with somethin' better if you want to save your necks.'

By this Darien was convinced the trio could only be owlhoot. The guns and the faces proclaimed it. The one called Durling plainly believed that anyone found lurking in remote country like this without apparent good reason could only be some kind of enemy.

So he cleared his throat and risked telling them the truth. Their abbreviated story didn't take long to tell and when he was through their captors just stood studying them in silence in a way that was unnerving – when the taut quiet was shattered by a command from the preacher outlaw. Pointing to the cavern mouth, the man called Rev or The Reverend, sighed and took his rifle off full cock. He gestured upslope.

'Follow me,' he growled. 'Get moving!'

Side by side the captives led the way upwards with their armed escort at their heels. They managed to appear unconcerned but this was a hard pose to maintain when your mouth was dry and your legs shaky, and you had naked guns all but prodding your backbones.

They were jittery as hell. And it wasn't much consolation to think, 'Who wouldn't be?'

THREE

POSSE IN PURSUIT

Bart Skillmore took his job as sheriff of Bucksaw, Kell County, seriously. A sober man of middle age he'd been filling the sheriff's chair for several years in which time he'd established a reputation for fair play and honesty. He had also shown himself capable of dealing firmly with drunken ranch hands, wild hill men and anybody else who even threatened to break the law.

Skillmore was comfortable in his authority and had no serious faults anyone was aware of. Yet on that bright morning with the sun just climbing over Big John Hill and the citizens of the Kentucky hill town getting on with their affairs following the recent upheavals, why was the almost teetotal lawman reaching into his desk drawer for the flask he kept there? Again?

The lawman studied the flask for a long moment then raised his gaze to the window and the imposing spectacle of Big John Hill. Just a few miles north of that hill lay the sprawling acres and imposing headquarters buildings of Hogueville Ranch, home of the county's wealthiest family, still in mourning over the death of the Wiggs's only son Corey, shot dead during a bear hunt by Darien Pell, since fled to escape the wrath of the dead man's father, Hogue Wiggs.

At the time of the tragedy the sheriff had investigated and reached the conclusion that hot-headed Corey Wiggs had wrangled with Pell over a bear killed that fateful day, resulting in Wiggs firing the first shot with Pell then shooting him dead. In other words, Pell had acted in self-defense which was not a crime.

Or was it?

There were no eye-witnesses to the gunplay, and Wiggs had subsequently built up a damning case against Pell while at the same time every hand on the spread was out hunting for the 'murderer'.

But the lawman knew Pell well and believed the incident had taken place exactly as he and Slim Carroway attested.

Nowadays the sheriff was drinking from guilt because he had been unable to stand up against Wiggs who still had upwards of twenty men roaming the county in search of Pell for the killing of his son.

The lawman was ashamed of his inability to enforce justice as he saw it. So he drank and kept silent whenever the Wiggs affair came up. Until today.

The sheriff took a slug from the flask, stoppered it with a grunt then turned his swivel chair to face Beau Wilson and Hud Henshaw, co-owners of High Bluff Ranch and participants in the bear hunt which had culminated in the death of Corey Wiggs.

Following a period of guilty silence on the matter the ranchers had finally come today to disclose they had actually witnessed the Pell-Hogue-Wiggs incident that day, and after much soul-searching had found the courage to come forward and announce their willingness to appear before a court of law and so testify.

With Hogue Wiggs uppermost in his mind the nervous lawman had attempted to discourage them from this course of action without success. He did so again now. But the ranchers' consciences were giving them hell. They had suppressed vital information that might have protected an innocent man from false accusation by Hogue Wiggs, and now would not be swayed.

They demanded a coroner's investigation into the Wiggs death and if the sheriff failed to provide this they threatened to take their information to the magistrate at Basine.

It was a half-hour later before the ranchers quit the jailhouse, but only then after the sheriff finally agreed to initiate the formal hearing.

But he was lying. He knew he must first inform Wiggs what was afoot – his life could be at risk if he didn't. The moment the ranchers quit his office Bart Skillmore tipped the flask to his lips and drank seep. He was drunk before he had the courage to saddle up and head out for Wiggs's ranch.

Hogue Wiggs was a pale man no sun could redden for long. Husky once, the fifty-five-year-old king of the biggest cattle outfit in the region was gaunt from grief, further exacerbated by his manhunt for his only son's killer. Today, the beef baron sipped whiskey straight for the dry cough he'd developed since the sheriff saw him last.

Yet these were merely superficial changes as the sheriff soon realized when they sat opposite one another at the huge teak desk in the richly appointed study at Hogueville Ranch.

Always arrogant and intimidating, Wiggs appeared even more so than ever in the wake of his only son's death. So much so that the sheriff was forced to request a drink after delivering his information regarding his visit by the High Bluff

Ranch owners, Wilson and Henshaw.

Wiggs rang a bell and a servant appeared instantly to pour whiskey at a dark-timbered bar which ran the full length of the room's west wall.

Skillmore gulped it down but it didn't have the hoped-for effect due largely to the fact that his host rose and came around the desk to stand over him in silence.

Although nowhere near the physical presence he'd once been, the ailing cattle baron had developed into a truly menacing personality since the tragedy. This had a disturbing effect upon the sheriff of Bucksaw during that silent moment.

The silence extended while sweat oozed from the lawman's face and his hands began to tremble. In desperation he suddenly attempted to rise only to end up upon the floor when the rancher punched him in the face.

'My son was murdered, you pathetic apology for a lawman!' Hogue snarled as the dazed lawman struggled to his feet, all courage gone in the face of such passion. 'Now get out before I have you thrown out. Get back to town and do your job and convince those scum, Wilson and Henshaw, that if they persist with their dirty lies about my son they shall not survive. You think I won't or can't guarantee that? I just dealt with you, didn't I? So – go!'

The sheriff was a broken man by the time he

reached town. He did exactly as ordered, yet struck trouble when Wilson and Henshaw originally proved stubborn when he delivered Wiggs's message. The two declared they would take their evidence farther as they'd already hinted they might should he fail to support them.

Two days later Henshaw's ranch house and buildings were set alight and burned to the ground. The arsonist was never identified but the two ranchers understood what had happened – and why. They made no further brave threats against Wiggs, leaving the range king free to concentrate solely on his ever-widening search for the man who'd slain his son. Wiggs vowed to find and kill Darien Pell if it took forever and few in the county now doubted he would do just that.

Moose Canyon was shaped by nature like a giant wheel with the ravines outlining the spokes while the hub was the raised flat area the party was now crossing.

Their captors guided them from the hub into an off-shoot canyon which they followed without speaking, with the heavy footsteps close behind. Soon they were approaching a wide-mouthed cave where burning brands lent the whole scene an almost welcoming glow.

Durling, the dangerous-looking man with low-slung Colts lolled against the mouth of the cavern, staring at them as The Reverend moved ahead to lead them inside.

Slim licked dry lips but Darien was feeling more aggressive than anything else. He was angered by the events that threatened to destroy the good life they'd been living before their world came crashing down. It didn't improve the way he felt to be taken prisoner by strangers and to have somebody poke him in the back whenever he slowed.

They passed by a low cooking-fire in the center of the cavern and entered an area lined with glossy animal hides and smelling of cooking meat and whiskey, to be halted where firelight flickered eerily over stone walls. All was silent for a time before another figure appeared in the the shadows and said, 'What the Sam Heck you got there, Connie boy?'

'Them two hicks that we figured must be tailin' us, Mack,' Connie Gaillard replied, bringing them to a stop. 'They claim they're just driftin' about, doin' a little huntin' and fishin'. They look too baby-faced to be John Laws, but who else could they be out here just where we happen to be holed up, huh?'

'Yes, yes, yes!' the indistinct figure replied strangely. When he moved forward into the light of the fire the prisoners saw he was of average height and lean frame. And though they could not see his face clearly they were conscious of being subjected to an intense and prolonged scrutiny.

'Well, they don't look too pesky to these old eyes,' the one they called Mack finally decided. 'All right, bring 'em in to the firelight so's we can all get a proper gander at 'em. C'mon, lads, move sharp.'

He seemed friendly enough, and as he moved ahead of them he was scratching himself and humming a tune, only breaking off to say, 'Yes, yesss!' several times. Darien found himself wondering if they hadn't maybe fallen into the hands of some strange maniac from the hills.

A bend in the tunnel brought them to the second fire, much bigger than the first.

The leader commanded attention. Mack, as they'd heard him referred to, stood with his back to them now as Durling reported on how they'd made contact, and whatever it was he reckoned they might be.

'Hmm, interesting,' this one summarized, still yet to be seen clearly. 'Very well, everyone sit and we'll have us a little drink while we try to decide just what breed of strange fish we might have caught today. Oh, yesss, yesss!'

'Sit!' Durling growled.

The two perched upon a rock slab facing the fire and Mack circled them now. 'This here is Connie Gaillard,' he told them, indicating the youthful giant who smiled at them as he propped his rifle against the stone wall. 'And the imposin' gentleman is The Reverend.' A deliberate pause, then, 'And I am Old Mack Dunn!' he announced as he moved to stand squarely before them in the firelight.

They stared, wondering where they'd heard that name. And gazing around from this strange one to study the others staring at them expressionlessly and in silence, couldn't help but wonder if their last hour had come.

Old Mack Dunn was a lean and easy-smiling man with an unruly head of hair and drooping red mustache. There was something about his appearance and movements that hinted at explosive energy. He had slightly protruding green eyes, was of average height and build with longer than usual arms and walked to and fro before them with a curious, forward-leaning gait like somebody eternally rushing someplace on urgent business.

He was doing this now while studying them intently as though committing them to lifetime memory.

Watching the way he moved, the partners wondered if that 'Old Mack' tag really applied. In the newspapers and the true-bills that offered varying rewards on the man's capture, he was always 'Old' Mack Dunn. Yet he could not have been a day over thirty-five, his tanned cheeks unlined and hair innocent of gray.

He wore clothes that looked as if he'd put on whatever was handy upon rising and wore a Colt revolver on his hip.

The only thing about him that seemed to support his notorious reputation was that big old Colt.

Darien scratched his head and frowned as he recalled how some newspapers often seemed to refer to this strange man as a 'gentle thief', whatever that might mean.

'Yes, yes!' the strange one said abruptly, as though, having inspected them he had now reached a decision. Darien and Slim traded glances, still unsure if they were in real danger or not as this odd one kept circling the area while everybody else was still. 'Well, what are you called, lads, and what's your story? I reckon you'd have to have one to explain why you were caught wandering around these badlands and running the risk of getting yourselves shot up.'

They swallowed at that. Were they going to be killed after all? But now the strange man chuckled and, they thought, surely nobody acted this way if they had murder on their mind?

Darien finally found his voice and briefly began recounting the circumstances of Corey Wiggs's violent death. Old Mack listened intently, punctuating his narrative with the occasional 'yess!', and nodding his head yet without actually interrupting.

When Darien finally fell silent the outlaw began pacing around the fire with his hands clasped behind his back and his head thrusting ahead.

'Well, what do you say, Reverend?' he demanded at last, halting before the tall man in the grey suit.

'I sense these lads speak only the truth,' came the unhesitating reply. The voice fitted the man's appearance. It was deep and solemn. 'It appears plain they have suffered grave injustice at the hands of this rich rogue, Wiggs. I can understand any man's grief at the loss of a son, but it seems this was a case of self-defense, pure and simple. Yet now this man has used the power of his wealth and position as mayor to set these boys outside the law.'

The Reverend sounded to the captives more like a judge or schoolmaster than any outlaw. He even smiled encouragingly at them as Old Mack circled the fire one more time before returning to them with a sudden rush of energy.

'Well, if I have it right, lads, you are outlaws now, men without rights or privileges – and as such the just target for any man's gun?'

This made them edgy again. But Slim Carroway spoke up, 'Sure we are. We've been living like mavericks ever since we quit the hills. It's been hell.'

'We were just planning to hole up out here to hell and gone away from everybody until Hogue Wiggs quit hunting for us,' Darien affirmed.

'And what next?' the outlaw wanted to know.

The two shrugged and looked at one another. They hadn't had time to work out future plans while simply trying to stay alive.

'I guess in time we would be thinking of heading west – cross the Mississippi,' Darien said finally.

'And do what there?'

'Work, I guess. Change our names, grow beards, get jobs.'

'Kentucky's Wanted posters show up out West too, you know?'

Slim slumped at this and looked at Darien. 'No, we didn't know. We ain't all that well up on this outlawing business yet.'

'If this Wiggs varmint is like you say he'll flood the country with so many reward true bills that you might be lucky to last a month before someone grabs you for the money. But maybe you're exaggeratin' things. Could be he wouldn't hang you if you were caught and brought back to the county, after all? He might just lock you up for ten years and let it go at that?'

They shook their heads in unison. They knew Hogue Wiggs and these people didn't. Knew he'd hound them to hell and back. They believed this if they believed anything.

Darien said as much then slumped and ran his hands through his hair. He was exhausted from running and hiding and having no place safe to go. He looked older than his years when he turned back to their captors – if that was what they were.

'You know,' he said after a silence, 'I guess we owe you fellers for not shooting us on sight. I reckon you've got to be outlaws, while we could have been law, anybody. So it's only fair on our part to make sure you know where we stand. Wiggs will hunt us wherever we go. If he was to come on to us with you, he'd likely deal with you the same way he would with us. . . .'

'Hey, don't you fret about us old boys, Darry,' Mack cut in. 'I got E.J. Durling in charge of the lookouts and I reckon he could handle any fifty cowboy possemen and hogswillers who might happen to show up all by his lonesome – him and that big .45 of his'n.'

'He sure looked mighty dangerous,' Slim remarked soberly.

'Yes, yes. But you don't have to fret about him,' Mack said. 'He's on your side, like me . . . least I guess we're on your side, haven't quite made my mind up yet.'

'But . . . but you believe us?' Darien asked anxiously.

Old Mack shrugged, then hunkered down and spread his hands.

'OK, maybe you've leveled with us and I'm rarely wrong judging a man. For the time being I'm going to trust you and play straight with you. Reverend, tell these lads how things are with us – after all they've just told us about possemen and all.'

The Reverend nodded solemnly. But as he rose and cleared his throat a sudden disturbance arose from beyond the caves. Instantly hands went to gunbutts and Darry and Slim were awed by their speedy reaction. Taking their prisoners with them, every hardcase was outside the cave with a gun in his fist well by the time a scout came down from the higher slopes at the gallop.

The rider reported sighting what could be a posse heading their way some two miles below the hideout. Everybody looked at Old Mack who 'harrumphed' noisily a few times then turned back to his prisoners. He spoke straight.

'Could be your possemen, eh, boys?' he speculated. They nodded warily and he said, 'Yesss!' then cracked his knuckles and struck a pose.

'We could whip them if we wanted but we don't want no shootin' match right now. So we'll ride – show 'em our dust. No arguments, this could be serious. Everybody go saddle up.'

It was impressive to see how the gang packed and loaded up within mere minutes. Old Mack came bustling across to where Darry and Slim stood uncertainly by their horses. 'So – we're pushing west. You fellers gotta mind to ride with us a spell?'

They stared, astonished by the offer and uncertain. Darien felt this was a huge decision that might prove irrevocable. Riding with outlaws could be tantamount to conceding that, dim as their prospects certainly were, they could be turning their backs on any slim hope of reclaiming their old free life forever if they allied themselves with such as these.

Such a giant step to take. Yet in the end it was surely Old Mack's swaggering personality and easy amiability that helped sway him.

Darian glanced at Slim who hesitated, then nodded and grinned; and so the giant step was taken.

'Be proud to,' he said simply, and the deal was sealed as they ran for their horses.

Half an hour's circuitous riding brought them once more into open country where there was a whispering ripple of wind in the high pines and the moon gliding down the channels between fleecy high clouds as they raced across the Razorback. Then down along gradual mountain slopes and onwards through the mist-pockets in shrouded gullies and then mile upon mile of needle-matted trails beneath tall black pines. Moonset flared and died hours later as they forded Ramsay's River and climbed up into wild country again.

In time Darien and Slim were half-forgetting the hardships they'd shared in the high lonesome along with the night of the black bear, the killing and their flight from Bucksaw. All forgotten in the excitement of the present. The Old Mack Gang rode like the wind and although the pards prided themselves on their own horsemanship they found it a challenge to maintain the fierce pace and not drop behind.

And every mile from his position far out in front, Old Mack sat in his saddle as easy as a Comanche buck and bawled snatches of trail songs in a cracked baritone, every so often hipping around in his saddle to glance back and laugh like they were all just a bunch of innocent everyday citizens heading off for an impromptu picnic in the country.

Dawn found them a hundred miles from Bucksaw, the long trail stretching behind them devoid of life.

FOUR

RIDING WITH THE GANG

They didn't really get to know their new trail pards until well into the following day.

All night long, then on through the soft morning, they rode to cross the Misty Mountains and later swam nervous mounts across the growling dark swirl of Ramsay's River. Then it was hard and fast through the tumbling low hills of Jethro County to reach at last the great river flats of the Mississippi.

'We've shook 'em off easy as a hound dog shucking fleas!' Old Mack boasted, check-reining his roan atop a crest above the river. 'Time for chow and a smoke.' He winked at the young fugitives. 'You fellers just ain't never ate until you've tried The Reverend's johnny cakes.'

He was right.

Sprawled out lazily in the dappled shade of an ancient magnolia the gang downed hotcakes and side meat with hominy grits with voracious appetites, then tasted coffee so good they realized they'd never consumed genuine honest-to-God coffee before.

The four-man bunch ate heartily with the exception of The Reverend who restricted himself to one huge mug of Java with a cigar while gazing out over the big river with his lips moving silently to his secret thoughts.

The runaways from Kell County had encountered some wild and strange men back in Bucksaw from time to time, and even the mountain town itself had its fair share of eccentrics and oddballs. Yet it was plain this bunch was totally different than anybody encountered before, and from the outset Darien and Slim sensed they'd been meant to cross trails with the Old Mack Gang. Their reputations as desperadoes along with their distinctive personalities, highlighted by their seeming disregard for both danger and the long arm of the law, had an almost hypnotic effect on the two – for a time at least.

So the two just sat and smoked and exchanged big grins while being formally introduced then coming to know their new trail pards – if that was really what they were.

They couldn't be sure of this yet as they silently studied their new acquaintances one by one. . . .

Connie Gaillard was the young giant with great barn door shoulders and eyes as gentle as a saint. He moved about like a man eternally weary yet his herculean body radiated immense power. His twang was broader even than Old Mack's and you could almost smell the cracker hills of Georgia whenever he spoke.

He told them he'd been in prison from age eleven until he was twenty and in the years since had been riding the owlhoot. Darien and Slim believed him when he assured them he would never see the inside of any jailhouse again in his lifetime, however long that might last.

'Old Connie killed his own paw,' Mack confided to Darien later. 'Seems the old man comes home one night with a skinful and starts in beating up on Connie's maw. Connie went out to the woodpile and brung back a two-edged axe. When the lawdogs showed up they found the old man had been cut clear in half, and that was how come he got to spend all those growing years behind bars while you boys would have been out skylarking.'

Mack paused to shake his head soberly. 'He's got a heart big as Texas but nobody should never want to rile him up, no siree.'

Darien tried to imagine what it would be like to spend your youth in a cage of steel and stone.

Then there was The Reverend. As quiet and grave as Connie was loquacious, this tall and angular gentleman with the fine head of silver hair that gave the final touch of distinction to his stately looks and bearing, The Reverend wore black broadcloth with a four-in-hand tie along with a Colt .45 on the hip worn butt-forwards, gunslinger style.

Nobody, not even Old Mack himself, knew anything of The Reverend's background. He was a man who loved to talk but never touched on his earlier life in that rich and educated voice. In a side pocket The Reverend carried a leather-bound copy of the Bible and every night in camp read a passage before turning in, and nobody from Old Mack down ever interrupted.

E.J. Durling was a hawk-faced man with a black mustache who preferred his own company. With his tied-down six-shooter and piercing eyes it was impossible to mistake him for what he was. 'Gunfighter' was stamped all over this one in big print. Of the bunch, the gunslinger was the one Darien warmed to the least and the feeling seemed mutual. Durling chose to treat the two with a cold-eyed indifference which was how it would remain – until the days of hate began.

When everyone had spelled for an hour beneath

the giant magnolias, Mack abruptly rose, grunting and scratching, to stare back the way they had come for a time before focusing upon the river, that great, outpouring channel of life that was the Mississippi.

He stood there for some time further, muttering 'Yes, yes, yesss!' to himself as though congratulating the Creator on a job well done in putting on such a fine day for himself personally – Old Mack.

'Of course you all understand,' he boomed out suddenly, gesturing wildly, 'that this here is the greatest and even the *only* genuine river in the entire world and she's been rollin' through these parts long before Columbus was out of short pants . . . and it'll still be rolling when all of us misfits are long gone and forgot. Uh-huh, oh yeah! No doubt about it, this is what a man can honestly call a river!'

Darien and Slim exchanged wondering glances. They were still growing accustomed to the leader's many eccentricities, his boisterous enthusiasms and wordy commentaries on anything that captured his attention. Today a river, tomorrow it might be hailstorms or a new fashion in women's bonnets.

Characteristically, Mack dropped rivers to switch to the subject of travel. Their own travel. He immediately began hustling around barking orders and grabbing up gear like they didn't have a second to spare. 'Right, lads, it's time to get moving – right now and immediately – yessiree! There's law behind us somewhere and a million unmapped miles for us to get lost in on the other side. So leave us get across this grandaddy of all rivers, and I mean now!'

There were no objections. All immediately began breaking camp, saddling their mounts and packing on the gear with none half as speedy or impatient as Old Mack himself.

At last ready for the trail, Darien and Slim stood together by their horses. Slim winked and grinned when Mack zoomed by with an armful of gear and still barking orders.

'Ain't he the limit?' he chuckled. 'Glory knows where he's taking us now, but you know something? I reckon that us stumbling on to this bunch might prove our first real break since quitting home – mebbe the best thing that could have happened. Hell knows where we're going but I reckon you can bet it's going to be different, maybe even exciting.'

'You could be right,' Darien responded. He fitted boot to stirrup iron and swung astride when Old Mack vaulted into the saddle with the agility of a race jockey and bawled 'Westward . . . Ho!' then led the way off at the trot. 'In fact, I'm almost dead sure of it,' Darien laughed, and used his spurs.

*

It was twilight when they reached the ferry station five miles up river. The ferry master and a pair of sodbuster passengers studied the six-man bunch nervously, staring at all the guns. But Mack immediately adopted the guise of a government revenuer, ranting and raving against the wickedness of all hill folks and how he had big plans to play hell with all the lawless whiskey-makers across the river.

The masquerade was so expert it convinced all on board that the bunch must be legitimate revenuers – not the intimidating gang, they'd taken them for at first glance.

Slim winked at Darien as they led their mounts on to the deck, jerked his head in Mack's direction.

'Ain't he the limit, Darry? I sure never met anybody like him back home. Hell knows where we're going now, but I've a hunch it sure won't bore us none.'

'You could be right about that, pard. In fact I'm sure of it.'

As the ferry pulled away from the levee, Darien stood alone by the railing, gazing back.

The light was fading fast now, the great blue mountains in the east dimming as the day was dying. So much had happened so fast that at times this strange new life didn't seem real. He thought of Betty Lou and his mother . . . and of Corey

Wiggs lying dead in the moonlight – the vengeful father.

Would he ever see home again?

Maybe the bullet that cut Corey down would sever him forever from the old easy life in the smoky hills and valleys, which until just one week ago had been the only life he knew.

He turned to face West, staring into his new life, while Old Mack stood above him at the prow with the captain extolling the virtues of steam over sail as a method of marine propulsion.

E.J. Durling stood by himself at the safety railing watching the dark waters slide by, while Slim and Connie yarned quietly over by the horse stalls. The Reverend was up at the prow, straight-backed and with chin raised and hands clasped behind him in a way suggesting he might start in delivering a sermon any moment now.

The ferry, a black silhouette against the burnished sheen of the water, wheeled its way confidently across the bosom of the Mississippi to skirt a low mangrove island then nosed in for the bank.

Oil flares lit the levee on the west side. Mack paid the toll fee and they rode away from the landing with curious eyes following them until they disappeared into the darkness.

The partners had no real notion where they were headed other than that it was west-bound.

And that was enough. When on solid ground once again Mack Dunn led them confidently away along a series of darkened trails to break eventually into the open country higher up.

At times they glimpsed the lights of distant towns on either side but never ventured too near. Soon the scent of the river was completely gone behind them and the stars flared with a brighter light.

Darien grinned at the way Slim was soaking it all up – this new life they were living like pilgrims.

They finally made camp on a windy knoll overlooking an immense valley studded by the glow-worm dots of scattered villages. Old Mack crossed to them with his hunched-up, headlong stride. He had a mouth full of biscuit and a mug of coffee in his hand.

'Still set on stickin' on with us?' he wanted to know. 'You're over the Miss safe and sound now, so's you can make your own ways now if you've a mind.'

They traded glances before Slim said, 'Reckon we'd admire to travel with you, Mack, sir . . . if you'll have us. Maybe I can't speak for Darrie, but that's my sentiments.'

Mack glanced at Darien expectantly. Darien paused only for the briefest moment, then nodded. 'Guess that's how I feel too.'

*

In the year that followed it might have seemed that there must be several Old Mack gangs roaming the owlhoot trails of the West. Riding like demons and seemingly impossible to run down, they swept through Kansas, Texas, New Mexico, Arizona, Nevada, the Utah Tertritory then back through New Mexico and into Texas again.

Banks, stages, gold shipments, trains, private citizens – anyplace where hard money was to be found proved fair game. The robberies were well planned and smoothly executed. The bunch hit fast and hard and were mostly long gone well before the sheer shock of their attack had passed.

The Reverend and Old Mack planned every detail of each operation between them, and many were the proposals they rejected because of the danger to themselves or, strangely enough, to others.

Mack had a maxim that you only ever fired a shot if you found yourself staring down a gun barrel at ten feet range or less. Anything less threatening than this you were expected to deal with without gunplay, and he personally set the example all had to follow.

The partners saw him support his own rules one blistering July day in Durango when E.J. Durling looked ready to blast a stage passenger who cursed him and called him a 'gutless rogue dog!' Before Durling could shoot, Mack laid his gun barrel across his temple and knocked him cold, then calmly toted him off along with the loot.

There were nerve-tingling times such as when they all sat their horses deep in the black moonshadow of heavy shade trees, listening to the nearing sound of a lumbering stage . . . then their swift explosion from cover and the bewildered expressions of passengers and crews as they encircled the coach with naked guns bawling, 'Bail up!'

These were days of danger and excitement to fire the blood. Of mad midnight flights through forests or across moonlit desert plains with enraged riders in pursuit; hair-raising brushes with lawmen, possemen, bounty hunters, vigilantes . . . of days and weeks wandering the wilder places of the West like kings with laughter always close, Old Mack still calling the tune and gold burning a hole in your pants pockets – most times.

But it wasn't all excitement and easy successes, and there were plenty occasions when they found themselves in full flight from outraged peace officers, or endless days and nights in the saddle with their whole bodies aching with fatigue and frequently with vengeful bullets whistling close through sagebrush and timber.

But such times were often offset by lazy days in El Paso or Tucson where they holed up to rest, blow their money and have fun – simple, harmless fun.

As time went by Darien and Slim rarely paused to question their new way of life. Had they done so they most likely would have agreed that, since they had been forced on to the owlhoot for crimes they'd never committed, they might as well enjoy the outlaw life, with the wide West as their private stamping ground.

Yet their roles in the holdups and suchlike were virtually innocent always – Old Mack saw to that.

Rather than embracing the owlhoot way of life as they might have done with another gang, they found their niche from the outset and nothing changed during that year.

Right from their first meeting Old Mack had been impressed by their horse skills. They'd been brought up amongst horses, were riding before they could properly walk, bought and sold horses as youths and might well have been successful horse breeders had not fate intervened.

Mack decided the gang needed specialized hostlers based upon the knowledge that swift flight – and the quality of their horses – more often than not in the wake of a stick-up, could often mean the difference between success and failure.

So the horses and their upkeep became their job. They were paid for it, were excellent at it, and Old Mack and The Reverend were able to congratulate one another on doing at least one good deed and saving two fine young men, as Old

Mack liked to boast in his cups, 'From a life of crime'.

Whether or not the law would look upon their activities in that benevolent light should the gang fall into the hands of the marshals one day, was unclear. But it salved Old Mack's conscience, while they remained with the gang, who provided a shield of safety for the runaways should danger from their past ever threaten.

But their job was neither totally innocent nor without its dangers.

They might get to hold the horses while a bank was being plundered, or con some fool with money into wandering down a dark alley where somebody as tough as E.J. Durling or crafty as The Reverend would be waiting to relieve them of their spare change and maybe scare the hell out of them – just for the fun of it.

Why they'd been admitted to the bunch or where it was all going to lead were questions that seemed less important as the days and weeks went by. To hear Old Mack ramble on sometimes you got the notion he'd simply taken a shine to them and simply let them tag along where they'd be protected should the Hogue Wiggs threat ever become a reality out here.

From time to time newspaper accounts kept the runaways in touch with events in Kentucky, and it was from these reports that they were able to trace the activities of Hogue Wiggs.

They had realized early on during their exile that the Wiggs threat would never simply fade away and disappear. Both from hearsay and newspaper reports they learned that Wiggs was almost never at his ranch but rather was continually on the trail with a bunch of commercial manhunters, trailsmen and guns-for-hire who were making serious money assisting the rich man in his hunt for his son's killers.

Many believed that Wiggs would eventually weary of the massive effort and cost of his blood quest, yet this did not happen. From time to time the fugitives heard that Wiggs's health was failing; that he'd collapsed on the trail in Kansas or Missouri; that even his original sympathizers had wearied of supporting him. But the one item that never made the headlines was that Hogue Wiggs had quit.

But awareness of their possible danger had little effect upon the two he wanted to catch and kill. If their lives had been uprooted and they were destined to be cut off from home and kin and continued to ride with Old Mack Dunn and follow a life on the dodge, then so be it.

It was a dangerous life, an uncertain one, but not without its compensations.

For instance, they were never bored.

Once outside Sante Fe the bunch directed their

attention to a train which was suspected of carrying pay money for the troops out at at Fort Ambers.

Turned out there wasn't a single pay packet to be found on the entire train. But a woman passenger chose the exact hour of the stick-up to give birth to her first child and Mack immediately assumed the role of midwife, barking orders and instructions to everybody, including the bewildered train guards.

The woman, wife of an army officer at the nearby fort, was so grateful to Mack for his assistance that she promised to name the child after him. He was so overwhelmed by this he immediately took up a collection at gunpoint from the passengers which he presented to the new mother along with a formal speech to mark the event.

Later, an eastern newspaper would dub the outlaw leader 'Gentleman Mack', but the name never really caught on.

Two days following the train incident Mack got drunk and held up three stages on one five-mile stretch of the Sante Fe-Hogue City trail to ensure that nobody got the idea he might be turning soft.

There were many such experiences yet there were also other very different times when sudden death rode at the stirrup of each rider and only skill, courage, luck and Mack Dunn's leadership lay between them and the rope or the bullet.

In a tiny one-bank town in Arizona, a gutsy bank teller reached a sneak gun and put a bullet through The Reverend's right arm before Connie brought him down with a bag of silver dollars against his head.

The Reverend's wound first appeared to heal rapidly before it suddenly broke out, evil-smelling and angry-looking. In their camp high in the Superstition Mountains the arm worsened and after three days of intense pain The Reverend instructed Mack to sharpen up his knife and get ready to amputate.

Instead, Mack saddled up and rode thirty miles to Phoenix where he kidnapped the town's leading physician and had him back in camp by sun-up.

Both outraged and scared, the good doctor went to work on the infected arm with Mack zooming around, boiling water, rolling bandages, jumping at the medico's every request and administering large amounts of rye whiskey to the patient as required.

During the whole episode Mack treated the doctor with great courtesy which convinced the man he wasn't nearly as dangerous as he'd been led to believe. He suggested that upon his return to civilization he might publicize the incident and Mack's distinctive role in it in order to show him in a better light. Mack agreed it seemed a noble notion, yet felt obliged to promise that if the limb failed to heal as hoped, he would seek out the doctor and shoot him, which terrified the man and he never mentioned the incident to anybody again, ever.

Despite his paternal attitude toward them all, Mack Dunn could be flint-hard when he had to be.

In Nevada, Connie's carelessness in mending a saddle girth on Durling's mount resulted in the gunfighter tumbling to ground with a posse pounding close behind when the patchwork gave.

It was only due to the fact that the entire posse turned turtle and hightailed when the gang rounded as one to come back for Durling, that avoided what would surely have been a bloody showdown.

Mack rode the miles to the hideout in total silence. Upon arrival he dismounted and strode directly across to Gaillard, who outweighed him by seventy muscular pounds, and still without a word hauled off and punched him in the mouth.

Connie went down but was up again straight off with blood trickling down his jaw and hand on six-gun. Yet he didn't strike back and later apologized for his carelessness. Later that same night Mack broke out a bottle of stolen French brandy and the whole bunch got at first happy and later maudlin drunk, with nobody retiring until sunrise.

That was the type of man that was Old Mack Dunn.

It was around this time that Darien began to realize that Mack filled the role of a parent for him, and likely did the same for Slim.

So they fitted into the outlaw band and never questioned why they were kept on without getting involved in the robberies. It seemed as if Old Mack regarded them like the sons he might never have. For their part there was no momentous decision to embrace the owlhoot as a way of life. They simply felt at home wandering the West with this oddly mixed bunch of characters – all home and safe.

There were few feelings of guilt due to the fact they were never involved in the dangerous stuff and the odd jobs they were given saw them merely minding the horses or keeping watch for lawmen while the gang cleaned out the bank or stole the horses. At times it felt as if they were acting out roles on a stage with blanks in the guns of the John Laws and a tacit agreement between lawmen and outlaws to return all money and goods after the game was over.

That was life in the Old Mack Gang and not even Mack himself could predict how long it might last.

FIVE

HEADING FOR KANSAS

Even at the end of another gruelling day of long miles and false leads in a country far from home, the rancher slept but fitfully. That night, with the wind moaning in the cedars and the campfire burning low at their feet, the new man kept turning his head to watch the tall, gaunt figure pacing to and fro over by the remuda.

'He sure must've been crazy about that son of his you told me about, I figger?' he muttered to one of the few who had been with Wiggs from the beginning, the ramrod of the giant ranch. 'All this time and still a-grievin'.'

'Things ain't always as they seem. . . .'

The new man stared across the flames at Jim Prince. 'What's that mean, top?'

Prince stabbed at the coals with a stick. He was worn ragged by the endless miles, the evil weather, the lack of success on the manhunt. Only exhaustion tempted him to speak his mind and somehow he felt he should – just this weary once. . . .

'He never cared a cuss for his son . . . none of us did. He was a whinin' loser all his life, mainly I always reckoned because the boss treated him so bad.' He gestured at the distant figure. 'If anythin' keeps Wiggs awake nights it's knowin' he was never a father's bootlace . . . so now he figures he might feel better if he squares accounts with the man who shot him.'

'Well . . . I'll be damned.'

'So will he, I reckon, when he gets to meet his Maker. . . .' The ramrod paused and straightened his shoulders as though suddenly aware of where a cold night and brutal exhaustion had led him. 'Better forget I said anythin', boy. I—'

He broke off on realizing Wiggs was coming toward them. Yet the man walked right by without even glancing their way, his face pale and ghost-like in the fireglow.

The new hand shuddered. 'You don't have to worry about me, top.' He paused to draw his slicker over his shoulders as a cold drizzle came down. 'He gives me the shudders, y'know. When do you reckon he's gonna realize we ain't never gonna find that Pell feller, and get back just to raisin' beef and stayin' to home?'

'When Pell's dead.'

'You mean . . . not before?'

'No chance. That's what guilt can do to a man, boy, so I'm learnin'.'

They fell silent at that, the fire crackled garrulously and the cold rain came down. They could see the shadowy figure circling the campsite and the new man almost felt sorry for Darien Pell, having anybody like Wiggs with his money, power and hate clinging like a burr to his trail.

'Riders comin', Ma!'

'*Coming!* How many times do I have to tell you not to drop your Gs, young lady!'

'They're still a-coming,' Phoebe responded, pumping up the swing by tucking her chubby legs under as she rose back, then kicking forward vigorously to give her the momentum to climb ever higher until she could finally see over the tops of the trees. 'Could be trouble!'

Clucking her tongue impatiently, Ma Pell emerged from her laundry and shaded her eyes, staring off down the trail. 'I don't see nobody.'

'They're still coming.'

'Are you being smart, young lady?'

Before Phoebe could respond a low drumbeat of hoofs reached the house and a short time later a bunch of riders came swinging into sight beneath the trees. They cut their pace as they closed in upon the house.

'Sure wish Darry was here,' the child said when she realized who they were. She rose high, was swinging back down as the riders slowed to a walk and approached. 'What do you think they want, Ma?'

'Guess we'll find out soon enough.'

Ma Pell was a hard woman to ruffle. Large and stately with her own brand of dignity, she was expressionless as she watched the horsemen reign in. Just one of their number came forward as far as her clothes line.

'Yes?' Her tone was neutral, neither friendly nor hostile.

The man she both hated and feared raised a kerchief to his mouth and coughed. The valley's most powerful citizen had returned to the county just the day before and they were shocked by his appearance, so grey and gaunt. Shocked, but not sympathetic as they watched him rein in at the head of his riders, eyes glittering in the shadow of his weathered hat as his gaze drifted over his surrounds.

He cleared his throat. 'Where is he?'
'Who?'

86

Hogue Wiggs lifted his jaw and fixed her with a cold eye. 'Don't make this any more difficult than it has to be. What have you heard of your son?'

'You mean the one you want to kill?'

The big man's eyes glittered as he shifted his weight in the saddle. Nobody who knew him expected Wiggs to relent in his manhunt for Darien Pell, despite the fact that a year had passed without word or sign of either him or Slim Carroway. Most every week there were rumors of a lead someplace, but by the following week these had always been disproven. Then new whispers circulated.

'The one who will face justice for his bloody crime!' he corrected, less composed now. 'Where is he hiding?'

It wasn't his first visit and doubtless wouldn't be the last. There were constant rumors of possible sightings of the runaways some time back, but such incidents had been dwindling as the cold season gripped hard.

Ma's response was characteristic.

'You men are trespassing—' she began but broke off as Wiggs heeled his horse toward her. He reined in, looming above her, his features almost colorless due to either anger or ill health – it was hard to tell which.

'I warn you, woman, when I catch your murderous son and see him hanged, should I discover he was assisted by you at any time I shall take it to the law and see you thrown into prison where you rightly belong. So consider that while I repeat my query – where are they hiding?'

Her response was unexpected. 'You don't look at all well, Mr Wiggs. Matter of fact you appear downright poorly.' She nodded sagely. 'Must be all the hate you've got inside you. Some say that hate can bring a body down as quick as the colic—'

'I was hoping you'd show more sense,' Wiggs shouted. 'You could reveal where he is and bring an end to all of this.' He heeled his mount around, then twisted in the saddle to glare back. 'But seeing as you plainly have no intention of acting rationally let me tell you what's in store for your murdering offspring.' He indicated his riders. 'There's rumors they ran west . . . like the curs they are. I'm setting out west again at daybreak with a dozen fresh trackers and trailsmen and won't be returning until I have your son either in ropes or in a casket, preferably the latter! Ho!'

At his shout the riders kicked into a lope and he led them back the way they'd come. As the dust settled slowly all eyes turned to Ma Pell, who looked deeply thoughtful.

They expected an outburst but she surprised them all with her calm.

'Diseased by hate, that evil man,' she said soberly. 'He's aged ten years since I saw him last, and by his appearance he would do better to hunt up a good doctor instead of hounding two innocent boys across the country.'

All including little Phoebe studied Ma Pell in sober silence, for most anything she ever said was accepted here. By this, everybody in the county knew how Hogue Wiggs had spent his every waking hour since the death of his son, covering often vast distances afield in his obsessive hunt for the fugitives. Today he'd resembled a man heading for collapse from exhaustion if he didn't ease up, yet it was plain he had no intention of doing that.

There was little talk after the horsemen were gone. For if it had not achieved anything else the visit had convinced everyone that the manhunt for Darien and Slim was unlikely to end before either Wiggs or their boys were dead.

The porch door creaked open and Mack strolled out on to the wide porch.

'Mind if I join you, son?' he asked Darien, seated on the edge of the veranda with legs dangling, attending to his Colt .45.

Darien grinned and indicated the battered rocker. 'Help yourself.'

Mack lowered himself into the chair and set it rocking to and fro, its creaking a relaxing sound in the quiet morning.

The bunch was spending some lazy days in a

nameless town which was little more than a saloon, hotel, livery stables and blacksmith's shop. A coal mine several miles west supplied the towners with employment, and its great appeal for the bunch was the absence of a law office.

After a time, Mack's chair ceased creaking and he leaned forwards. 'Tolerably nice country, eh, boy?'

'Not bad, I guess.'

'But of course, not a patch on Kansas.'

'Is that so?'

'You bet. Of course, when I say Kansas, what I'm really talking about is Kansas City.'

Darien was wary straight off, for if there was one topic Old Mack Dunn could overdo at times, it was Kansas City.

So he said, 'Let me tell you about some of the cities in Kentucky while—'

'Seen 'em all,' the other interrupted. 'Nothing. Compared to KC that is. I can assure you that if you were to take away Kansas City and the Mississippi River, why the West would be nothin' more than a whole mess of buffalo tracks, Apache wickiups and maybe the odd Texas Ranger huntin' for badmen like yours truly.'

'If you say so, Mack,' Darien smiled. 'But talking about the Rangers, is it true they've got a company someplace detailed just to run you down?'

'Who told you that?'

'I heard The Reverend and Connie talking about it once.'

'They talk too much.'

'Is it true?'

'Yeah, it is. And that riles me, I tell you, boy. Why, I know fellers ridin' the owlhoot like me who'd sell their own mothers for a dime and scalp 'em for a dollar. Now I don't like to bad name a man, but when I hear of the carryin's on of gunners like John Wesley Hardin and his like, it just don't seem right for the marshals to have old Redgold assigned special to me and the boys.'

'Well, we're not exactly ideal citizens, are we, Mack?'

Mack scowled. 'I don't go much on that *we*.'

Darien dropped his air of easy banter. 'I don't understand, Mack. I figured Slim and me would be accepted as part of the gang by now.'

'Don't get me wrong, Darry boy. You two young fellers handle yourselves bettern than any your age I've ever struck, yes siree. But—'

'But what?'

'Well . . . what I'm thinkin', I guess, is . . . why don't you boys just quit, I guess.'

'Quit?'

'Forget believin' you're outlaws, is what. Hell, you two ain't even got your faces on any true bills out here, and I'll see to it you won't neither. Nobody knows you're alive so you've nothin' to

91

fear. OK, so you mightn't be able to return home. But out here you got a million square miles to roam around in, start a new life, plant roots and make something of yourselves. You've got what it takes to do that.' A pause, then, 'Matter of fact you remind me plenty of myself at your age. Only thing, I didn't have a smart old bastard like I am now any place around to steer me straight.'

'So . . . that's why you've watched over me like an old mother hen? Because I remind you of yourself?'

'I never planned to make that noticeable.'

'Well, I've noticed. And I reckon Durling has too, and he doesn't like it. Matter of fact I don't reckon he thinks we should be ridin' with you at all.'

Mack was very sober as he paused to frame his response.

'Forget Durling. The bunch needs him to survive, but he's different from the others – harder, colder, meaner, by God! But necessary as hell, believe me.' A pause, then, 'And while I'm on my bandwagon, boy, you shouldn't listen too much to your pard, neither.'

Darien straightened sharply. 'Slim? What's wrong with Slim?'

'He *likes* the life you two fell into with us. That's the difference.' He held up his hands as Darien made to protest. 'Let it ride, son. It's you I don't want to see wind up at my age runnin' like a fox bein' chased by a relay of hound dogs all your life.'

There was silence for a time as Darien digested what had been said. At last he shrugged. 'Well, all I ever really wanted to do was marry my girl, buy a piece of bottom land and raise cows and horse . . . mainly horses.'

'Glad to hear it. And you got the touch with horses right enough. So why not think about shuckin' this life, buyin' yourself a piece of land and sendin' for that gal back home you keep moonin' about?'

'I wish it was that simple. . . .' Darien was silent for a moment, thinking of the kinfolk that needed him. Then he spoke sharply. 'But if you're so full of good advice why didn't you give yourself a dose of the same and settle down?'

Old Mack turned rueful and massaged his brow with a distant look in his eye now.

'You know . . . there was a girl once.' He paused, then added emphatically, 'A *real* girl. It was way more years than I want to recall back in Kansas City – only the greatest city in the entire West. She was only small, but prettier than a whole field of Texas bluebonnets and a smile that made you think of Christmas and the sun sparklin' on fresh snow. Well, we fell in love and I promised to marry her. Only thing, I had one last job I had to see to. It went wrong, I was chased around Colorado for a year and when I got back it was to learn she'd quit the country – took a boat!' He paused. 'She'd simply tired of waitin' for me. You want somethin' like that to happen to you?'

It was quiet for a while on the battered old porch, a good time for one man to look back and for the other to think ahead. Darien was simply thinking about his girl back home in the hills of Kentucky. But Mack's reminiscing on the great love of his life – and how it blossomed and then died – got him excited again about something that would surely take his mind off such things. And it's name just happened to be – Kansas City!

'By glory! That's what I need right now – what we all of us need,' Mack suddenly decided, jumping to his feet. 'We'll forget stickin' up penny ante banks or liftin' lousy cows for a while,' he said, his face now alive with animation. 'Damnation! Thieves and runners need good times as much as anybody else, and where better to find them than in the finest city in the country? OK, not a moment to lose, Darrie boy. Go drag the boys out of the saloon and give 'em the news. This time next week we'll be in Kansas City – and you can look a lot happier about that if you'll give her a try.'

Darien thought he was joking until next day's dawn found them setting out on the first twenty-mile leg of the long trail to Kansas City, Kansas.

SIX

THIS MAN IS DANGEROUS

Mack was first abroad next morning and was soon striding about bawling orders with baggy pants flapping as he rushed to and fro at a furious pace, eyes alight with an excitement nobody had seen in quite a time.

'Yes, yes, yes!' he was saying. 'A full reunion of the old Denver Gang, Blackleg Tom, Julian Ketchell, Slim Donovan, Johnny Dollar, Timbertop McCue. Then all you jokers – The Reverend, Connie, E.J. – and the two boys. Hoo-hah! I'm here to tell you that Kansas City will be the greatest get-together ever. They don't know what's about to hit them!'

For everybody else it was far too early on a grey morning to get enthusiastic about anything, but they responded even so. Durling stood watch on a high spot while they readied for the trail, for while this was considered safe country far from the beaten path, when you were part of the notorious Old Mack Gang you took all the precautions. Just in case.

'The final, absolute party. . . .' Darien heard the familiar voice announce from the back porch where he was hauling his saddle down from the kit shelf. 'How did I ever get to stay away from the old hometown so long. . . .'

He was grinning when he made his way across the dim yard. He began to whistle until a voice sounded from the gloom of the hay barn.

'Cut that row! No need to tell the whole town we're moving out!'

He propped. He knew the voice. Moments later the unmistakable silhouette of E.J. Durling moved into view. He halted with thumbs hooked in shell belt, head tilted to one side in characteristic pose.

'Somethin' on your mind?' Darien said.

'Just a word of advice.'

'Don't recall askin' for it.'

Durling approached. The two had never hit it off since the new men first linked up with the bunch. They had never clashed openly but had come close to it more than once. Inwardly, Darien had always reckoned Durling lacked the class to ride with Old Mack, while Durling made no secret of the fact that he considered the new recruits unworthy to ride with the bunch.

The gunman halted again. 'This is a dumb idea of Mack's, hill boy. Kansas City, I'm talking about. He's got a stack of friends there – but just as many more who hate his guts. I'm gonna be expected to watch his back the whole time and I won't be riding herd on you two teacher's pets of his at the same time. So, why don't you take a hint and drop out now?'

Darien was stung but wouldn't let it show. Though in no way afraid of the gunfighter, he didn't care to mess with him any either. What was the point? They were all part of the Old Mack Gang and would surely encounter enough trouble here to satisfy anybody on the trail sooner or later. So why wrangle amongst themselves?

'I'll quit if Mack says, Durling,' he said, making to step by. 'Not before.'

A powerful hand clamped his right bicep. 'Look, junior, if you won't take a hint I just might have to hammer it into you—'

'Hey! What in tarnal is going on out here?'

The shout saw Durling break his grip and step back a pace. Darien glanced over his shoulder to see the tall figure of The Reverend descending the steps with his warbag slung over one shoulder.

'Shucks, wasn't nothing, Reverend,' Darien grinned. 'Skylarkin', I guess you'd call it.'

'Yeah,' Durling muttered. 'Just high spirits bubbling over.'

The Reverend appeared to accept this and Darien continued on his way. He didn't give the incident much thought, which might have been just as well considering what lay not twenty-four hours ahead along the trail to Kansas City.

The night caught the tail end of the moon and before the silver light was gone the six horsemen splashed across the crooked creek to ride into Coopertown.

'Chow!' muttered Connie Gaillard, hunched up against the high country chill.

'And warmed-up blankets,' breathed Slim Carroway, drawing his jacket collar up around his ears.

The others rode on in silence as they clop-hoofed down the lifeless main stem then turned in at the lighted building with the battered sign saying LIQUOR creaking in the wind above the door.

By the time the first round of drinks had been taken there were signs the gang was warming up after the ten-hour ride that had taken them to the top of Spanish Range. Even so they were in no mood for conversation, not even with the unexpectedly pretty blonde girl behind the counter who served up drinks with smiling efficiency.

For her part the girl was genuinely pleased to see the strangers, two or three of whom she considered quite handsome, while all six appeared relaxed and almost genial. Or at least in comparison with her last batch of customers passing through, they did.

The new arrivals didn't learn about this earlier group which had stopped over briefly here on their way north-west, until the following morning at breakfast.

In characteristic fashion Old Mack was making harmless chit-chat to the servant-girls while they ate, when one enquired if they were connected with the other party.

'And what party would that be, beautiful?' Mack asked idly, savaging a warm bun.

'The rich feller,' they were told. 'Came through with a bunch of riders, so he did. Come from east someplace . . . did you catch where, Mavis?'

Mavis was a plain honey-blonde and obviously impressed by E.J. Durling in his tailored leather jacket. 'Er, Wicks or Willis – something like that. Kind of lary that one was, all windblown and fierce-eyed . . . and askin' questions all the time and—'

'Wiggs!' her companion broke in. 'That was his name, and he—'

'*Wiggs?*'

It was Darien Pell who spoke and everyone turned to see him rising slowly from his chair, appearing suddenly pale in that light. 'Did you say Wiggs?' he said sharply.

'Uh-huh,' the pretty one affirmed. 'Mr Wiggs and party, it said on the register. They only stopped over a few hours and—'

'What did he look like?' Slim broke in, also on his feet now.

'Why, a tall, gaunt man with black hair and kind of piercing eyes. About fifty or so I'd say. Never smiled, and kept staring around like he was expecting to see someone familiar. Asked a power of questions too, so he did.'

'About what?' Darien demanded.

Two girls shrugged and the third nodded. 'Said they had business with two fellers from the east . . . two young fellers with names like . . . well, who remembers names?'

'Carroway was one,' the other girl recalled. 'He didn't say why but he sure seemed to want to meet up with these fellers real bad.'

The pards traded stares, stunned and alarmed. By the time they'd asked more questions there was no doubt in anyone's mind that it had been Hogue Wiggs from Kentucky who'd passed through here just a day previously. Wiggs and a large party were still hunting them after all this time and so far from home!

This hit hard and Darien knew he would look every bit as stunned as Slim by the time Old Mack finally caught on what had happened. Characteristically, he promptly settled them down in his own inimitable way and began to talk in his easy knowing way.

'Boys, boys,' he smiled around a freshly lighted cigar, 'It ain't the end of the world. So, a breath of the past whispers close. Happens all the time with me.' He gestured airily and went on to spin tales of close shaves and hair-raising experiences until most everybody was feeling relaxed and reassured again.

But it was still disturbing to realize the hunt for them had continued after all this time, and for a brief moment had drawn quite close. Darien had hoped Wiggs might have given up, or even that he might've perished someplace on the trails, in which case they'd likely return home and set about clearing their names.

But Mack was right to be cheerful, he knew. Danger had brushed close but had vanished again into the north – while the gang was *en route* for Kansas City. They were traveling in almost opposite directions, so what was there to fret about?

Mack eventually led them out into the bright mid-morning and they loped off due east.

*

101

Mack was first up that morning three days and many miles later, eager and energetic as ever as he paced up and down before the campfire. He was making his plans for Kansas City and waking everybody up with his rambling chatter.

First to join him at the fire was Durling, already clean-shaven and characteristically expressionless as he stretched with supple grace.

'Howdy, boy, howdy,' Mack greeted enthusiastically. 'So, how come you're up and about so early?'

'Nobody sleeps when you're on the rantan, Mack,' the gunman said soberly.

'I'm sorry, but I was just tellin' Darry here what he can expect when we hit the City and meet up with the old bunch. Which promises to be one hell of a better time than stickin' up stages and gettin' shot at for a spell, right?'

'If you say so.' Durling eyed Darien as he rose from his bedroll with a six-gun in his fist. 'Ready for action, eh, kid?' he said sarcastically. The fast gun resented Mack's refusal to permit Slim and Darien to be within a mile whenever they staged a hold-up or bank job to replenish their coffers.

Darien didn't look up. 'It's Mack.'

'Yessir,' Mack grinned. 'That old cutter was burred up some so I gave the boy the job of whippin' her into shape.' He shook his head. 'Never know when a man's gonna need a good

102

shooter, you know.'

'That's so,' Durling said with an edge to his voice. '*Somebody* has to be ready to burn a little powder in an outfit like this.'

Darien's head lifted sharply. 'That a crack at me, Durling?'

A shrug of broad shoulders. 'Why, I never knew you weren't doin' your share of the serious work.'

'I do what I'm told,' he snapped back, which was nothing but the truth, and Mack still kept the two in the background if there was any prospect of powder burning.

Mack interrupted sharply. 'Steady, you two. A day like this is too fine for squallin'.'

'He's always makin' cracks,' Darien accused. 'A man can grow tired of that.'

'Like I'm tired of you and your pard gettin' a free ride with the rest of us takin' the risks, hillbilly!'

'Cut it!' Mack snapped and they knew they had gone far enough. 'Look, E.J., you just gotta remember – if I wanna keep the young 'uns out of the thick of things that's it. I'm the boss and you'll just treat 'em civil. Understand me, boy?'

'Whatever you say, Mack,' the gunfighter murmured, then turned and strolled away with the sun upon his bare head and striking points of light from the gun snug in its holster.

Mack burped and drilled a finger into his ear.

103

He squinted after the receding figure.

'He ain't always at his best mornin's, old E.J.,' he drawled.

'He's not at his best any time as I see it,' Darien remarked.

Mack chuckled.

'You two are like a pair of gamecocks. I saw it the first day that you showed up, you two would never hit it off. Could be you're too much alike to be pards.'

'You reckon I'm like Durling?'

Mack held up his hands in mock defence. 'Easy there, son. What I mean is that both of you are prideful as well as mighty slick with a shooter. Guess competition betwixt two like that ain't so unusual.'

'Durling's a killer,' Darien said harshly, surprised by his own words. Until that moment he'd not realized his dislike for the gunman ran so deep.

'Well, guess I can't deny old E.J. is a handy man with a cutter.'

Darien felt he should leave it at that but found he could not.

'Why do you keep ridin' with him, Mack? He's not the same as you or The Reverend or Connie. You're outlaws, sure, but real men. Durling is just a butcher. I reckon a man like that with his hot gun could touch off something that could get the rest of us wiped out.'

Mack fell silent and leaned against a boulder, watching as Darien gave a final polish to the six-gun in his hand. He passed the piece across and Old Mack held it up to the early sunlight, admiring its mirror sheen.

'You did a good job, Darry, I'm beholden to you.' He toyed with the weapon a moment longer, then rubbed it with his sleeve and said, '*That's* why I keep E.J. on, boy.'

'I don't understand.'

'The reason I gave you this here weapon to clean is simple, boy. You see, I ain't never shot a man in my life, but, damnitall, the life I lead, I know a man should at least *look* the part.' He paused and shook his head as though puzzled anew by an old mystery.

'You mean you keep Durling on to do your gunfightin' for you?'

'Somethin' like that.'

'But Connie and The Reverend. . . ?'

'Are top hands with their cutters and with the guts to back 'em up, yessir.'

Darrie frowned, then grinned. 'You know, Mack, right from the start I figgered you were different. Guess I just didn't know how different, was all.' ——

'So, you don't direspect me on account I ain't no shootin' specialist?' the other chuckled.

'No chance. I suppose, thinkin' on it, I respect

you more.'

Mack liked that. Yet he was very sober as he hooked thumbs in shell belt and put on a frown.

'A word of warnin', boy. Don't mess with that tall Texan. He's a top gun and a good trail pard, but mean. . . .' He nodded and moved across to the fire, where he added quietly, 'He'd kill you quick if you gave him reason, and there wouldn't be a damn thing I could do to stop him.'

With that he walked off to where it was quiet under a big sky. After a time Darien went off to roust Slim out of the blankets just as the sun was climbing the sky. It looked like a good day coming on, the sort of day when you should forget things that likely didn't matter . . . and just ride and think about making the miles to Kansas City. . . .

SEVEN

HERE COME
THE RANGERS

Darien and Slim never lost sight of the reality of Wiggs's obsession to run them down. Yet to discover that the rancher's manhunt was still operating at full strength so far west of Kentucky after all this time, was a jolt. It made a man wonder if the cattle baron was still even sane.

All the more reason why Mack's notion to go to Kansas City sounded so welcome, and the bunch struck out in high spirits with good horses under them to cross the mighty grassland prairies of Kansas.

Until suddenly it was neither pretty nor peaceful any more.

The bunch reckoned they'd shaken off Redgold's Rangers six weeks earlier back at Derringer Springs in the shadow of Queen of Hearts Mountain. So it came as a brutal shock when they set out that clear morning from Shane River only to realize they were being followed.

Redgold's Rangers didn't even enter anybody's mind. At first. Darien's hunch was that it might prove to be the Wiggs posse, yet he couldn't figure how that outfit could have possibly picked up their trail. Eventually The Reverend volunteered to drop back to find out who it might be, and didn't rejoin the bunch until late that same night where they camped around a low fire in a secluded cave. The news he brought back wasn't as bad as they'd feared. It was worse!

Redgold's Rangers, whom they had shaken off their trail out at Derringer Springs weeks before, were now back on their trail less than ten miles behind!

Consternation reigned, at first. Yet Old Mack's calm ensured there was no panic. He totally rejected Durling's suggestion – get in first with guns.

Old Mack quashed that, for the Mack of these Kansas days was a vastly changed man, who'd privately come to the conclusion that his wild free-wheeling life was drawing to a close at last. The Rangers had always posed a threat, yet now

Redgold's latest appearance had dramatically upped the stakes in the game by picking up their scent when they all believed they'd left none.

But Mack's response was much like always – cool and unexpected. He immediately announced they would head north, which initially touched off opposition as the gang favoured pressing straight on for Kansas City and shaking their tail *en route.*

Mack proved inflexible. He reckoned the threat was serious, insisted the wild and largely unpopulated north to be their safest refuge at the moment – and anyone who didn't agree with him was free to quit.

That snuffed out the dissent. Fast.

An hour later saw six horsemen galloping across the Karnack tundra under a sullen moon with the north star fixed between their horses' ears.

It would be a full week later before a bunch of gun-hung strangers lined themselves up before a row of cold beers in a seedy Kansas cowtown ten miles farther east to drink to the fact that Redgold and his Rangers had been bested. Again.

Draining their glasses fast they tramped out boisterously to the tie-rack, swung up and once again pointed their horses' noses back in the direction of Kansas City.

Captain Redgold was a top manhunter who hated failure the way a rat hates red pepper. His bitter mood was obvious to all as he stood lean and poker-faced listening to his long-haired scout deliver his report some twelve hours later.

Their quarry had eluded them. Again.

The day he'd been summoned to Ranger Headquarters to learn he was personally assigned the task of running down the fugitives from Kentucky involved in the Wiggs murder case, the manhunter had felt both eager and confident in his ability to achieve success, as he'd done so many times before.

Not this time.

The Rangers had received a positive early lead on their quarry and vigorously followed it up, only to fail as they'd failed against the Old Mack Gang before. Now the officer had been summoned to headquarters for yet another 'please explain'.

Proud and resentful, he took his calling-down the way a good officer should, thanked his men for their efforts, then disappeared to get drunk.

He succeeded.

Yet the first light of day still saw him rousting out his bugler, who in turn aroused the Rangers whom Redgold led back on the trails before the sun was properly clear of the horizon. The captain had vowed to run Old Mack down if it meant riding to the ends of the earth, never realizing in those early, confident days that he might well have to be prepared to do just that.

*

Darien and Slim were conducted on a tour of his childhood hometown by a weirdly disguised Mack Dunn.

Today he sported a bed-of-flowers vest, a green hard-hitter bowler hat with steel-framed spectacles with no glass in them, plus a flapping black, clawhammer coat.

He was so conspicuous a figure here on the streets of his youth that he attracted more attention than might have been the case had he strolled Central Square with a placard on his chest reading: I AM OLD MACK!

Even so the disguise achieved its purpose insofar as throughout the crazy week that ensued, nobody had recognized him. By that time Mack felt secure enough to ditch the disguise and allowed all the con men, dude gamblers, outlaws on the dodge and painted saloon women of his early years here welcome him home while still preserving his anonymity from the authorities.

At all hours of the day or night he was to be sighted hurrying from one saloon, café, gambling joint or speak-easy to another with one, two or even all of his wild bunch in tow. And was, for the moment, Kansas City's most unique attraction.

Mack made certain he saw everything, caught up with everybody and even managed somehow to

111

convince the law that, while admitting his name was Dunn, he was certainly not *the* Mack Dunn of outlaw notoriety. And because he was so aggressively on view and apparently harmless as he zoomed from saloon to gambling den to upstairs establishments operated by ladies with names like Blonde Bettina and Dime-A-Night Kate, they believed him!

For the bunch, the sprawling Kansan town proved as colorful and exciting as Mack had painted it to his gang over many a campfire during the wandering years. Unlike many western cities that had become squalid and down-at-heel under blistering heat and freezing winter rains, Kansas City was all vigour, bustle and character in that handful of days as they tagged along in his wake along the back alleys and main streets. They gaped at squalid slums and stared in awe at red brick mansions with manicured gardens.

'Yes, yes!' Mack enthused as they tramped through fruit markets and uphill to the greystone buildings of the ultra-rich cattle barons and railroad-tycoons. He halted once to question a little oriental man about some old friends, stunning him when he pressed a large bill into his hand for his trouble, then zoomed off to lead his pards through a night of excitement, high spirits, vast amounts of liquor, pretty women and stirring music – and a hell of a lot more they wouldn't be able to recall next day.

*

Dawn. The brutal reality of crippling hangovers, broken furniture, stogie butts stamped into the carpets and a neat pistol hole in the forehead of the stuffed moose above the saloon bar . . . furred tongues, regrets and recriminations.

But by this Mack had had his fill of nostalgia and was easily persuaded – in the grey, hungover light of early morning – that they should quit while the going was good. So they lurched raggedly into the streets and headed for the stables under the early sun, almost wilting under its impact in their debilitated condition.

Mack ran back once with coat-tails flapping and a twisted cigar clamped between his teeth to bid farewell to their hosts of the night before, succumbed to their insistence he linger for a goodbye shot of whiskey, then was roundly cursed for the delay by the bunch when he eventually got back and managed to mount up at his third attempt.

He led them off down the main street at the gallop waving his green bowler and bawling that he would be back – until the last clapboard shack fell behind.

Only then did he sober and brush back a tear. For only Old Mack knew he would never be back. This was his farewell tour of old haunts and

113

nobody knew the secret plans for the future his merry blue eyes concealed. . . .

Once clear of town he tipped his hat over his eyes and promptly dozed off in the saddle after calling to Darien, 'Lead the way, boy, as you're the only one sober. Lead the way south – and watch out for Rangers – ho! ho!'

This was said in jest and was treated as such. Yet five miles south, with Kansas City fading behind in the morning mist, the joke turned sour – and bloody. The gang forded a shallow stream and were climbing the long wooded rise beyond when half a mile ahead a troop of horsemen suddenly swept into view.

It was a sizable squadron of uniformed riders who initially seemed as startled by the bunch as they were by them. Momentarily both groups reined to a halt, the Old Mack gang squinting in hungover uncertainty up the long slope until alarm first struck the teetotal Reverend.

'I don't believe it!' he gasped disbelievingly. 'That there is Redgold and his Rangers!'

Mack, swaying sleepily in the saddle mere moments earlier, snapped bolt upright in the saddle, fully alert in a moment. In back of him, Darien was able to pick out the tall figure of Ranger boss Redgold, identifiable by the brass-buttoned blue tunic he wore. A triumphant shout rose from the Rangers' ranks as Redgold led them forward at the gallop, their excited shouts ringing loud across the valley, weapons glinting in the sunlight.

'Ride!' roared Mack, raking spur against horsehide. 'Ride like you never done before!'

Every man hit the gallop in moments but for Durling who hung back to challenge defiantly at the enemy. Before Darien was aware of it Slim had impulsively turned back to go galloping off to the gunman's side where both began blasting at the uniformed enemy.

It was a crazy thing to do, if heroic.

Mere moments later, Slim Caroway's horse was struck. The animal crashed down dead and Carroway was hurled clear. He came up blasting as Durling, taking advantage of the diversion he had caused, suddenly raked with steel to go storming off at a racing gallop with six-gun now holstered, leaning low over the animal's neck.

Darien couldn't believe Slim had been abandoned by the very man he'd turned back to assist. Realizing what had happened, Carroway hurled a curse after the fleeing gunman then began to run, taking huge bounding strides and working his Colt furiously until a storm of Ranger lead chopped him down.

Even at distance a horrified Darien could tell his friend was dead, even before he stopped rolling. Chilled, horrified by the murderous speed of it all, he had no option but to rake with spur and went storming after the bunch to ride as never before, the gang's well-rested mounts eventually leaving the played-out Ranger horses far behind in their dust.

He rode on without once looking back on the blackest day of his life.

The sheriff of Bucksaw glanced up from his desk at the sound of boot-heels from the jailhouse porch. At first glance he thought the man who entered to be a stranger – yet somebody who still appeared to feel he was entitled to barge straight into a law office without even knocking and approach the desk as if he had the authority to do so.

Yet surely there was something familiar about this tall, gaunt figure up close he thought irritably, rising. Wasn't there?

The man swept off his travel-stained hat and the lawman gasped. 'By glory – Mr Wiggs! But . . . but—'

He broke off. He'd been about to remark on how poorly his midday visitor appeared but realized that would be an understatement. He'd heard of the manic manhunt being conducted by the master of Hogueville Ranch, an obsession believed to have already taken him halfway across America and back.

The sheriff backed up a step before his visitor's fixed glare.

'Anything new come to hand during my absence, Skillmore?'

The lawman cleared his throat as his visitor remove his hat. He saw immediately that the Hogueville Ranch boss had aged a decade, with hollowed cheeks, sunken eyes and his always severe mouth now reduced to a bitter razor slash.

'Er ... nothing new concerning the people you've been hunting—'

'What about the family? Have you been keeping that brood of bastards under close watch during my absence, as instructed?'

'Why, yeah ... sure I have,' Skillmore lied, swallowing painfully. 'Again, nothing, Mr Wiggs. It's my opinion that Pell and Carroway must have fled the country by now—'

'I don't recall asking for your opinion—'

The rancher fell silent and steadied himself against a corner of the desk. He drew the back of his hand across his mouth and for a moment appeared distracted by the faded pictures of long-dead desperadoes gazing stonily down upon him from smoke-darkened walls. He turned back sharply as one of his riders entered and threw a half-salute.

'Nothing from the saloons, Mr Wiggs,' he reported. 'Like before, it seems Pell ain't made no

117

contact with home since we was back here last . . . and with rumours of Carroway's death and all, I guess that—'

'Shut up and get out!' Wiggs grated. He glared at the lawman who felt he needed a stiff drink real bad. 'Well, what information on Henshaw and Wilson? And don't try and protect those lying whoremasters either, badgeman. Are they still threatening to take their lies about how my son died to the District Attorney during my absence?'

'N-not to my knowledge, Mr Wiggs—'

'Have they withdrawn their filthy allegations concerning the murder?'

'Not officially as far as I know.'

Another man entered at that point, also travel-stained and leg-weary. The ranch ramrod had spent months criss-crossing the West with a second bunch of hands which the Wiggs spread could not really afford to be without.

'Well?' Wiggs barked.

'Er, Doc Simpson's outside, boss. Seems he heard you was back and lookin' kinda poorly, so he thought he might . . . well, you know . . . look you over and mebbe prescribe somethin' for your—'

'Get out, you fool!' The rancher gestured violently and shouted, 'Order every man to mount immediately. We ride out in five minutes.'

The man disappeared and the sheriff felt genuinely concerned.

118

'Mr Wiggs, surely you're not thinking of leaving again so soon? Aren't you afraid that you might—'

'Afraid? Damn you, my single fear in life is that the bloody murderer of my son might die or be killed before I can find and kill him – personally!'

He was gone, leaving his final words seemingly echoing around the room: 'Kill him! Kill him! Kill him!'

The sound of horses starting up drowned out the clatter the sheriff raised in opening a desk drawer and hauling forth a bottle of bourbon. He uncorked and took a long pull of the whiskey, shuddered and shook yet found a brief strength.

'If you kill young Darry *you*'ll be the murderer, Wiggs!' he said. But it was said very softly so nobody might overhear.

Somehow Darien was able to stay on top of his rage until that grey day one week later when something seemed to snap inside him. Without a word to anyone he buckled on his gun and was making for Durling's tent when suddenly Old Mack appeared from no place to stand squarely before him, calm and amiable yet commanding as always.

'No, son!' he said, reaching out and plucking the .45 from Darien's holster. 'That gunshark could kill you three times over before you even cleared leather . . . and I'd be left to bury another fine friend that I can't afford to lose.'

'Slim risked his life to save him and Durling threw him to the wolves, Mack. He's got it comin'.'

'I won't argue with you on that. But think on this, boy. How do *I* feel about what happened? You and your pard would never have been in any shoot-out but that you tagged along with me. It was rotten, it was dirty, and I hate Durling's guts for it. But I also need him, son – and on top of that I'm not going to stand by and watch him kill another good man like you. I couldn't live with two deaths on my conscience, so if you won't step back for your own sake, do it for mine.'

It was a titanic struggle for Darien to overcome a rage more fierce than any he'd ever known – yet somehow he finally triumphed – for Old Mack's sake. He gave his word he'd leave the killer be. For now.

Old Mack was willing to settle for that.

EIGHT

THE HEART
OF TEXAS

Texas again. . . .

Darien sat his saddle twisting a smoke into shape as he watched Old Mack swagger across the dusty white street heading for the mail office of this nameless town.

At a rough count this would be about the fourth or fifth Texas town the gang had visited riding south, in order that their leader might go check for mail. Nobody knew what Mack was expecting but whatever it was it appeared he'd not received it to date.

Darien drew hungrily on his cigarette and gusted smoke into the sky. He reckoned he'd understood Mack's sudden impulse several days back that saw the bunch sweep swiftly southwards down across the mighty Lone Star State from the north – at first. Slim's death, the ongoing tension between himself and Durling along with learning that Redgold's Rangers had made a public boast to bag the entire Old Mack Bunch within the month . . . it was surely a time of uncertainty. There seemed to be an ongoing sense of turmoil and threatening change in the very air, which contributed to feelings of confusion and tension. And in Mack's case, mystery.

Today Darien wasn't sure if he really understood anything anymore. For the farther south they struck – Dallas, Waco, San Antonio – the stranger Mack's behavior seemed to be. They all still grieved over Slim's death. Yet although Darien knew Old Mack was outraged at the time, the man appeared anything but down or depressed these days. The contrary. Adding to this mystery it appeared to Darien that the farther and faster south they journeyed, mostly skirting the bigger towns, and hearing the occasional rumor that Redgold and his Rangers had somehow picked up their scent again – the higher Mack's spirits seemed to climb.

Darien might have resented this but for the fact that Old Mack had never let him down and therefore warranted his trust. He reckoned that whatever lay behind the leader's high spirits as their headlong pace placed vast regions of the mighty Lone Star State behind them, was something he would understand – in time.

After Mack vanished inside the rickety unpainted building it grew quiet beneath the huge maple tree where the horses were tied. The day was blazing hot and everyone seemed to welcome the opportunity to relax in the shade except E.J. Durling. As usual the arrogant man of the gun stood apart with arms folded, his sneer seeming to have become permanent during their headlong southwards odyssey.

Never popular with the band, Durling's stakes had plummeted since Kansas. He was mostly isolated but it didn't appear to faze him. He kept a close eye on Darien, who had made no attempt to approach him since Mack had stepped in that day. Nobody knew what was going on behind that cast-iron face any more than they understood what it was that was so plainly invigorating their leader these days.

And why Mack's sudden interest in post offices anyway? Not even The Reverend could figure that one, and it was unusual for Mack not to confide in him.

Dunn reappeared abruptly across the road. All turned and stared for it was plain even at a distance there was a pronounced skip in his step now. And when he reached them he was chuckling and punching his palm with his fist – surely odd behaviour on a roasting Texas summer's day.

'What?' prompted Durling.

'Huh?' Mack grunted innocently, feeling for the makings.

'You look different, Mack,' put in Gaillard.

'You boys have been out in the sun too long.' Mack lit his smoke, stretched his arms overhead, squinted south. 'But I know the sure cure for that. The seaside.'

'What goddamn seaside?' someone wanted to know. 'There's only one I know within reach of here, and that's Galveston.'

'Galveston?' someone else echoed, looking a question at Mack.

'As fine a destination as you'll find this time of year anyplace,' Mack attested, vaulting nimbly into the saddle. 'So like they say in the shippin' towns . . . all aboard who's comin' aboard!' Then kicked his horse away leaving the bunch to make up their minds if they were prepared to continue on south or quit from sheer fatigue.

'A hell of a note!' commented Connie Gaillard, yet he was already making for his horse. 'Mighty strange,' agreed Darien, and followed. He called, 'OK, Mack, we'll go to Galveston.'

'Eventually,' came the distant response.

Everyone halted. 'What?' growled Durling.

124

'Funds,' Mack replied, pausing to allow them to catch up now. 'There's an operation to stage in Galveston and funds will be essential. Luckily I've kept one ear to the ground and know just where to make a withdrawal.'

Everyone began talking at once, demanding to know what was afoot. But Mack was terse now. 'You'll find out when we get there,' was as much as he would say, then kicked away.

It was testimony to their loyalty for Old Mack that every man eventually trailed him out of town and pointed their mounts south. Their attitude seemed to be, 'If you can't trust Old Mack, who could you trust?'

Nobody knew how Hogue Wiggs learned that his quarry had been sighted at last on a day that marked the third long week the manhunting party had been criss-crossing the south-west. Yet two days into the forced ride which he had led from Kansas the rancher approached the Texas border near Charleyville, and was leading them into the town, when the ranch ramrod began noticing the children on their way to school coming towards them, and how oddly they were behaving. Several of them gaped up at Wiggs astride his palomino mare, pointing and seemingly alarmed.

The riders expected the testy Wiggs to react to this. When it didn't happen a man kicked on ahead to draw abreast of the leader.

He saw immediately that Wiggs's gaunt face appeared devoid of all color and that his chin was resting upon his chest, as though he slept. Then very slowly he leaned sideways, his falling hat revealing the staring eyes before the dead man crashed to earth.

The party dismounted to encircle the motionless figure in silence.

It seemed a long time before a weary ranch rider coughed and looked across at the ramrod. 'Does this mean we can all go back home where we belong now, Top?'

'Why . . . why, yes, reckon it does at that,' the ramrod responded, clearing dust from his throat.

'Well, thank God for that,' a puncher said feelingly. And that would be the rich man's only epitaph.

Old Mack threw a fatherly arm around Darien's shoulders and guided him away from where the others sat eating in the shade on that milder midday. When he halted he rested hands on hips and stared him straight in the eye.

'You're still stickin' with us, boy,' he accused, yet with all the old affection. 'You want to tell me how come?'

Darien pretended not to understand. 'You're not trying to get rid of me, are you, Mack?'

126

There was no answering smile from the outlaw boss.

'You know what I mean. That newspaper we picked up yesterday was full of the news from Kentucky, trumpetin' about how everyone and his brother has come forward to talk up since Hogue died. Witnesses are ready to swear you killed Hogue's son in self-defense . . . seem to be fightin' to be heard.'

He paused to spread his hands.

'The truth of young Hogue's death is comin' out just like you told me it was from the first day we met. You're cleared as an innocent man, and free to go home. So what are you still doin' here down in south Texas with a no-account bunch like us?'

Darry had been expecting this ever since the news of Hogue's death came through. He was prepared for it.

'I mean to keep on with you to Galveston, Mack. I've got a hunch you're plannin' somethin' big down there and I aim to see what it is. I want us to part the right way and that seems the place to do it.'

Old Mack studied him closely from crafty blue eyes. Whether he believed him or not was difficult to tell.

'You never mention Durling these days, son,' he said pointedly and surprisingly. 'How come?'

Darien glanced away. Sometimes Old Mack was so sharp you could almost believe he could read your mind.

'He killed my buddy, Mack. Why would I want anythin' to do with that sonofa—' He cut himself off, forced a smile, shrugged. 'Look, only a few more days to Galveston. When we get there we'll have a big blowout and then I'll get on my hoss and head home for old Kentucky. Will you maybe rest easy then?'

'Mebbe.'

Darien grinned. 'Well, now you've finished grillin' me and what I'm doin' – what about you?'

'What about me?'

'Well, this bustin' your britches to get to the coast, for one. You've been tryin' to tell us how you've always wanted to see Galveston, Mack, but I can tell you're lyin' through your teeth. Now we're headin' there I know you're hatchin' somethin' big, I can tell. So why don't we do a deal? I'll tell you why I really want to get there if you level with me first.'

Old Mack glared, rested hands on hips, then burst out laughing.

'All right, damnit! Keep your lousy secret.' He abruptly poked Darien's chest with a hard fore-finger. 'But I've see you watchin' Durlin' when you think nobody's lookin', son, so I want you to keep clear of him now, and down in Galveston,

128

and as long as you're still with us. You got that clear?'

'Hell you nag, Mack. Are we goin' to chow down, or not?'

Mack slapped him on the back and started off at his usual furious pace. 'We eat,' he laughed and, tagging after him, Darien realized he'd never seen the man looking happier. He hoped to find out both the real reason behind this journey and Mack's high spirits before he did what he had long sworn to do.

Kill E.J. Durling.

Old Mack insisted he didn't really *want* to bail up a stage coach – but that he simply *must*.

'You're not makin' any sense, Mack,' The Reverend objected. 'A man either wants to do a thing or he don't—'

'No time to explain,' Mack cut him off, slurping down a mouthful of freshly brewed coffee at their trailside camp some place north of Galveston a week later. He paused to produce the letter he'd found awaiting him at the last post office between here and Galveston from inside his shirt. He scanned the contents yet again, grinned.

'Yessir,' he affirmed, slipping the envelope away once more. 'No two ways about it. Big dinero is needed and if I had time I'd surely try and come by it an easier way. But time and tide is against me,

I need fare money . . . er, cash, that is, and I guess I got to look for it to be on the four o'clock stage from Galveston comin' north in about a half hour.'

Blank stares all around. All this seemed almost out of character from Old Mack. Yet such was their level of trust in the man they'd followed so long, that after some musing and mutterings the decision was reached. They would bail up the pay stage for the mines – but Mack had better have good reason for doing so.

Mack promised to explain. Eventually. But right now he had a hold-up to organize, and straightaway began striding up and down the clearing barking instructions and waving his arms, not pausing until he came to Darien, who was at least as puzzled as everyone else.

'No time to explain, boy,' he insisted, not quite meeting his eye. 'But this has got to be done, believe me, so now you just disappear. Like always.'

Darien objected but was quickly overridden. Throughout the entire period he'd ridden with Mack, the leader had never permitted him or Slim to take part in any of their crimes. It was plain he wasn't about to alter this rule here on a nameless bend in the Galveston trail.

'I just don't figure,' he complained some time later when he and Gaillard lay sprawled behind a deadfall from which point they would eventually see the stage roll into sight. 'Mack don't hold up stages. What's he need dinero of a sudden for?'

'Your guess is as good as mine,' Gaillard replied. 'Hey! I hear wheels!'

NINE

THE TRAIL
LEADS SOUTH

The special stage of the Silver Fan Mining Company en route from Capitan to San Antonio carrying $11,000 worth of gold dust under heavy armed guard, was bailed up and robbed at Cripple Creek Crossing on 11 May, 1886.

The robbery was carried out by four armed and masked desperadoes who burst from concealment without warning from the heavily timbered growth surrounding the watercourse, brandishing guns.

Such was the abruptness of the attack that the escort was powerless to do anything but surrender, then watched helplessly as the precious dust cases were removed from the coach and lashed to the outlaws' saddles.

The whole incident was conducted with such speed and efficiency that it later led the authorities to believe that those responsible could only be a major outlaw gang, quite possibly from the North.

Having completed the job without a shot being fired the desperadoes vanished swiftly, leaving the escort to return to Capitan to face condemnation and likely dismissal.

But the authorities were not about to take this outrage lying down. Fortunately, it was known that the renowned Ranger Company under the command of Captain Ethan Redgold had reached Capitan two days later, hunting for a lead on a bunch of northern desperadoes. The account of the hold-up supplied by witnesses convinced the captain that the crime had all the earmarks of the old enemy he'd been pursuing so long, Old Mack and his bunch.

Following a brief rest period at Capitan the Rangers quit town at the gallop and headed south-west.

They made an impressive sight as they cleared the town limits, yet local hopes were not high. This far south, it was believed that Old Mack could never be caught and many were prepared to bet hard money that the wily desperado, whom so many secretly admired, would give the law the slip. Again.

Redgold was exhausted and angry. This showed plainly in the stiff way he sat his saddle while scouting to and fro across the limestone reaches with Scout Lefarge trailing behind at a respectful distance in blazing midday heat.

From time to time the officer would halt and raise binoculars to his eyes to scan the surrounding emptiness. He saw nothing of note and following each survey would jam the instrument back into the leather pouch slung from his belt and slog onwards in search of sign . . . any sign would do at this late stage.

From where the Rangers watched their commander in the shade cast by a towering granite butte it seemed plain he would find no sign now. The limestone here was hard enough to resist a blow from a pickaxe and would leave no sign even from a steel-shod horse's hoof.

Yet Redgold continued to plod to and fro in brain-boiling heat and there wasn't a man who didn't understand his obsessive behavior.

The tracks of their quarry had originally led south-west from the crime scene for several miles before abruptly swinging due south. The Rangers had followed the trail behind their leader in puzzlement for many miles, their confusion stemming from the fact that they knew there was nothing south of this region but a hundred miles of heat, dust and desert between themselves and the Mexican Gulf.

Eventually there was no sign to follow. The tracks had been leading inexplicably into the semi-desert when the winds had blown it away, so there was no sure guessing at the destination the crooks had in mind.

Standing apart from the others with his back resting against a towering butte, top scout Arnie Breen was frowning as he watched Redgold. This entire region was new to him and therefore he couldn't hazard a guess at the gang's destination either.

He turned as a Ranger strolled across, a shy, lanky fellow called Demogue with whom he'd struck up a casual friendship since joining the squad.

The man drew up in the shade and squinted against the glare that shimmered about the distant figures of Redgold and his off-sider.

'He's sure in a sweat about all this, ain't he?'

'Reckon so,' Breen replied. 'Can't say I blame him though.'

'S'pose not.'

Breen shaded his eyes and cut his gaze south as though trying to probe its secrets. But all he saw was an unbroken expanse of nothingness stretching away to be lost in the haze. Even in shade it was hot enough to make a lizard sweat.

'Ever been south of here?' he growled.

'Once, afore I joined up. Drove a bunch of beeves to the Gulf,' Demogue replied.

' What for?'

'For the shippin' crews. They're always starvin' for beef by the time they reach port from South America. They eat a mess of it while in port then salt away what's left to take back to sea with them.'

'Much of a port?'

'Galveston? Sure is. Wild, but kind of exciting.'

Breen straightened. 'That in reach of here?'

'Sure.' The man grinned. 'Easy to see this is your first time down in these parts.'

Breen barely heard. He was suddenly recalling how he'd read a newspaper account a year back that related how Old Mack Dunn had got drunk someplace and declared that one day he would finally quit the owlhoot and make it down to Galveston, and ship out to leave America behind forever.

Nobody had taken the piece seriously. Yet what if they were wrong? What if the coast was Mack's destination, for whatever reason? That could explain the reason behind the gang's southern journey and also make some sense out of the sign they'd been able to follow this far until it petered out.

From what Breen understood, Galveston didn't

boast the kind of big rich banks that might catch Mack's eye. He had the impression it was largely a melting pot of poor folks and gangs of brawling sailors plus an outsized law force which struggled to keep everybody in line. In short, a typical coastal town. And this posed the question: what attraction could this place hold for Old Mack – unless it *was* the sea itself?

'Say, where you goin' of a sudden, man?' Demogue called as Breen abruptly spun away and went striding off into the sun making for the remuda.

'To see Redgold!' Breen's reply carried back.

The squad had stopped off here to off-saddle and rub down their mounts in the shade. Breen's runty mustang was half-asleep on the remuda line, hip-shot and head-hanging in the heat. He mounted bareback and kicked into a trot under the sun, Redgold looking up curiously as he approached.

'What is it—'

'I could have a hunch where they went,' Breen announced, reining in and jumping down. 'How far is it to Galveston?'

'Huh?'

Breen talked fast and the more he did so the more likely his hunch seemed to look. To himself, that was; not in the eyes of his superior. So he had to argue long and hard before Redgold finally quit scoffing and began to listen. Yet due to the fact that he was hot, frustrated and still nagged by the fear that he might be forced to give this manhunt best, the officer was sarcastic when he said at last, 'Why didn't I figure this for myself? All these years on the owlhoot that criminal was simply just building up for the chance to sail away to South America. And what for – take up growing pineapples? I can see Old Mack doing that. The hell I can!'

'I'm serious!' Breen cut in. 'And just think. If I'm right it would finally make sense of why Mack's come this far . . . and is still pushing south. But of course if you want to dismiss it like—'

'All right, all right,' Redgold said placatingly. 'Don't get in a sweat.' He turned and stared south for a long moment, slowly relaxing before murmuring, 'I wonder. . . .'

'There's got to be a reason to justify this journey south. Won't you agree on that?'

'Near on a hundred miles . . . just on a hunch. . . .'

'Stronger than a hunch,' the scout persisted. 'Look, we both know Mack is double clever and crafty. You give me one good other reason why he'd tackle a journey like that from here to the coast if he wasn't planning to ship out?'

'All right, all right!' Redgold straightened in the saddle, stared south, nodded to himself then fixed Breen with a gimlet eye. 'Whatever motivates you . . . you just might have convinced me your figuring could be on target.' A brief pause, then, 'We'll do it.'

'Head south?'

By way of response, the officer hipped around in the saddle to beckon his lieutenant who'd been sitting his saddle some distance away while the two conferred.

'Go ready the troop to strike south,' he ordered.

'S-south, sir?'

'Are you hard of hearing, man? Yes, south – south to Galveston. Well, what are you waiting for? Get moving!'

'He thinks you're loco, er, sir,' Breen couldn't help remarking as the man hurried off.

'He could be right. But just remember. If you're wrong here – for whatever reason – I'll guarantee you'll regret it.'

He held up his hand as Breen made to respond.

'I've already made myself clear. Do you know if there's water available south of here?'

'There's a creek at Click River and a good seep at Antoine Springs.'

'Very well then, that's settled.' Redgold nodded briskly. 'Give the men the order to break camp.'

I wish I was twenty,
With kids of my own,
I'd let them miss school,
If they kept me in gin—

The song finished abruptly as the porch door banged open and Phoebe looked down from her high-climbing swing to see her mother standing on the stoop in her patched cotton dress, hands on hips and scowling.

'If I hear one more word of that disgusting song, young lady, I'll report you to Brother Herbert at Sunday School and you'll miss the Summer Picnic! Do you hear me?'

'Sorry, Ma.'

'And so you should be!'

The porch door banged shut and Phoebe was alone again with just her brother's old dog for company. She was silent for a time, swinging to and fro, then softly, softly sang her very favorite song, the one she'd composed herself;

Darry come home, Darry come home,
Wherever you wander, wherever you roam,
Darry come home,
Don't leave me alone.

She realized it felt so good just to hear the sound of his name spoken out loud here where everyone seemed to doubt he would ever be seen alive again, that she kicked and swung until she was almost touching the sky with her toes and could see the above the trees the road he would come down one day, some day . . . soon to find out

140

that the bad old man who'd lied about him was dead and gone and everyone now knew the real truth about how that man had died. . . .

Darry come home,
Oh Darry come home. . . .

Not even The Reverend was sure why Mack had set such a brutal pace to reach the sea, yet the moment they'd arrived he was tearing off someplace like all the hounds of hell were yapping at his heels. The Reverend was exhausted yet still felt obliged to trail after him and finally found himself outside a postal depot at Distote where Mack vanished inside then reappeared a short time later clutching yet another letter, his face animated.

Saddened and hurt by the secrecy, The Reverend concealed himself when Mack came swaggering by. He felt that maybe for the first time ever his old pard was keeping something from him.

Scout Lefarge was just a few hours out in his predictions for the time the journey south would take. The 7th Ranger Company reached Galveston in the early evening three days after quitting the limestone country at Capitan in the north.

The forced journey was testing yet the troop of both men and mounts were so trail-hardened from the preceding weeks manhunting that their destination was accomplished with only minor discomfort.

Spirits rose when they first glimpsed Galveston with the blue waters of the great gulf beyond. They made camp on a sandy beach on the western side of town. Here were shade trees, fresh water and a curious bunch of Mex kids who gathered around the trail-stained bunch whom they seemed sure were *bandidos*, with their six-guns and rifles.

Redgold gave the men permission to swim in the bay while he and his right-hander made for the heart of the city.

'We'll present ourselves to the local law,' he informed them. 'I've never heard of a Ranger troop visiting this place before so I guess we'll be in for some surprises.'

'Not as big a surprise as Mack and the boys will get,' burly Mason said optimistically.

Redgold's thoughts focused upon his quarry. He reckoned it was something Mack Dunn injected into any place he happened to be, this energy – a blast of turbulent air and sense of excitement he always seemed able to generate.

'Looks like the law office up ahead,' Redgold said eventually, and quickly turned his mount to lead the way across the street to a hitchrail which stood before a large, stone-fronted building with the legend US LAW OFFICE in bold black letters above the long front gallery.

They dismounted and climbed the steps together to enter the building.

An orderly showed them into the office of the post's marshal where Redgold presented his credentials. The beefy marshal with two six-shooters thrust through his belt looked even more like a desperado than some of the shady characters they'd encountered upon the streets. However, a few minutes' conversation revealed him as a keen-minded officer with real pride in the job his outfit was doing in keeping a lid on the brawling seaside city.

The man was astonished to find a member of the famed Texas Rangers in his town, was further startled by the suggestion that Old Mack Dunn could also be sharing the city's hospitality.

He even had a Wanted poster of Dunn on his wall and the ranger suppressed a weary grin on confronting the illustration of the desperado. Mack looked as if he were about to scratch himself and say, 'Yes, yesss!'

The marshal had no knowledge of the bunch's whereabouts but promised to put all his officers on full alert while reminding his visitor that Galveston was a large and sprawling city in which to conduct such a search.

Redgold thanked him shortly afterwards and they left.

The ranger's eyes wandered restless over the faces they encountered as they rode. He sighted so many different nationalities: American, Mexican, Chinese, Indian, African, Hispanics and a hodge-podge of strange faces and mannerisms, the origin of which he could only guess.

But he failed to sight the towering and dignified person of The Reverend or the impressively formidable features of the man of the gun, E.J. Durling.

He reached down and loosed the Colt in its scabbard, flexed the hand he'd trained so long for one task. He was as ready as he would ever be.

Later he visited a number of shipping houses to enquire on port movements. They learned that no ships had left for southern waters over the past twenty-four hours, which enhanced the possibility that Mack might still be here – waiting. During their journey south the Rangers had pushed horseflesh to the limit, while noting that the sign they encountered suggested that by contrast Old Mack had taken it in easy stages, plainly not fearing pursuit.

It was a little after nine when they emerged from one such house that Redgold spotted a shop displaying sweetmeats.

'A treat for the men,' he grinned at his offsider, and disappeared inside.

When Darien returned to the hideout on the backwater levee where the bunch was camped, he found it deserted. He was surprised but unconcerned. Doubt didn't raise its head until around midnight when the failure of the bunch to materialize first made him edgy, then suspicious and finally angry.

He spent several hours searching Galveston end to end and daybreak found him seated exhausted on a lonely pier jutting into the bay waters, facing the unthinkable.

He'd been dumped. Old Mack and those hard men he'd come to regard as true friends, had deserted him.

But why?

TEN

ADIOS MACK DUNN

A mystic wraith of fog lay over the brown sea waters that night – a sultry, steaming Galveston night with the unceasing hum in the air of a million cicadas.

Beneath the darkened black hulk of the levee it was a little cooler, with Gulf water lapping around hoary pylons and pale fish swirling to their deep destinations.

Across the way beyond the ghostly moss-trees, Galveston burned orange-bright. Out in the bay were dark ships, ghostly, fogbound Cereno ships with high Spanish balconies and ornamented poops – until you drew closer and realized they were just battered old freighters from Africa or New Orleans.

A strange moon rode high in the sky and ferry

fires glowed in the night. Negroes hummed and sang their spirituals upon an up-river levee as they toted their heavy burdens ashore.

E.J. Durling slapped a mosquito on his neck, his curse blending with the sound of the slap.

'The foul of tongue shall never enter the Kingdom,' intoned the voice of The Reverend from the surrounding gloom.

'Buffalo dust!' snapped Durling, and returned to his moody brooding.

'Yes, yes, yesss!' came yet another voice. 'Harrumph, hah, oh yes, indeed!'

This might have sounded like the disjointed mutterings of a fool to some but the outlaws knew it as simply the sounds of Old Mack Dunn awakening from a nap.

He emerged from a hammock slung between two pylons, scratched, yawned, hawked, ruffled his thatch then moved out beyond the levee shadow of their hideaway to the water's edge. The moon was pale yellow across the bay and fog tatters hung wraith-like all around. 'Ha, yes indeed! Yesss. . . .'

'You still reckon they'll come for you?' Durling wanted to know.

'Sure as sin, E.J.,' Dunn replied. 'All arrangements are final and complete and the money has been paid. Have no fear. The dinghy from off the freighter will arrive at this here levee at midnight on the dot and take us aboard the *Star of Brazil* with

147

promptitude. Then it will be farewell and good riddance for all posses and Rangers. So long Texas and also Kansas City . . . goodbye, so long and fare-thee-well. . . .'

His voice trailed away and just the way he looked they could tell he was thinking about Darien, and how he felt bad about deserting him after all their time together. But he knew he'd done the right thing. The next twelve hours could be fraught with uncertainty and danger as he attempted to board a ship for the south. He had enemies and when Redgold's Rangers had been sighted, he had known he couldn't risk the young life of a man he'd come to look upon like the son he'd never had.

'Sorry, boy,' he whispered to the night, and the lonesome toot of a bay ferry responded from the darkness.

Durling stared at the night sky, spoke over his shoulder. 'You reckon he'll go through with it? Sounds to me he's been talkin' about it so long that now the times's come he ain't as keen as he was, mebbe.'

The towering shape of The Reverend emerged from the gloom. He stared off after Mack's receding figure for a moment before answering.

'I believe he really means to go this time. Ever since he made the decision back in San Antonio, he's been heading south.'

The tall man paused, then decided he needed to say more, as much to review recent events in his own mind as to inform others. 'I finally realized a woman was behind Mack's journey south. It's an old flame he told me about once, and after Kansas he decided it was time to quit the game, but only if she would be waiting for him.'

He paused to see if everyone was paying attention. All were. He went on.

'He'd wrote to her on the trail, stopped off at every post station until he finally got the answer he wanted up at Distote that day. But right off he knew he had to get a bunch of dinero together that he'd need to finance the journey south and for him and his woman to live off down south. So we did the bank robbery. Everything hung on that and when it came off – well, there was nothing to stop us. The signals went out last night and all we gotta do is wait.'

'I'm sure as hell up to the craw with all this waitin'. I never was one to set about. The way I figure, a movin' target gets hit less often,' a deep voice growled from the shadows.

'Why don't you ride out, E.J.? You're not shipping out with Mack, and you've got your cut of the take. Get in some saddle time.'

Durling hooked thumbs in shell belt and stared straight ahead. 'I've a mind to do that. But I'm tippin' he'll change his mind at the last minute. Guess I wouldn't be surprised if we all of us ride away from Galveston together, Reverend.'

The Reverend clasped his jacket lapels and cleared his throat. His gaze played over the moon-dappled bay and his voice held a yearning note as he spoke.

'My soul hungers for peace, E.J. For too long I've tried to reconcile my nefarious trade with my conscience and have only succeeded in uncovering the depths of my hypocrisy. Perhaps away from America I could become once again a man of honor . . . forget I'd ever been a bloody rogue.'

Durling studied him closely. 'Damnit, you puzzle me, Reverend. I've ridden with you a mighty long spell, but I still don't know why you ride the owlhoot, even where you hail from.'

'Nor shall you, E.J.,' came the response that cancelled out further discussion on the topic.

A brief silence. A boat horn hooted away up the river and a dog yelped somewhere back toward town. Durling rolled a cigarette and applied a vesta to it.

'What if Mack changes his mind, Reverend? I know you're set on leavin'. What would you do if he did that?'

'Why, ride with him, of course.'

'You'd do that just for him?' Durling shook his

150

head. 'You know this is likely your last chance to quit, don't you? You're gettin' on, slowin' down and the lawdogs are barkin' louder every year. You'd likely get nabbed and hanged if you were to go on with it. You know that as well as me, so why would you stay on?'

The Reverend bent an imperious stare on the gunman. 'Because he is my brother, E.J. What better reason could a man have? Not a brother of the blood, but something far closer – a brother of the spirit.'

Durling lapsed into silence. He did not understand; friendships and relationships were beyond this merciless man of the guns. He dragged deeply on the cigarette and watched the smoke mingle with the wisping fogs.

The Reverend said quietly, 'And how about you, E.J.? Why have you stuck with Old Mack so long? Surely not because of warmth for the man?'

'And why shouldn't that be the reason?'

'I know you too well, that's why. At heart you're a loner who doesn't really need anybody ... correct?'

A thin stream of smoke trickled from Durling's lips. It seemed a long time before he replied, his voice a little odd.

'You're right, Reverend. I've stayed with Mack because I've needed him.'

'*You* need somebody?'

'Not friendship. No, I've never needed that. I just wanted him around to stop me goin' off the rails. I was always too hot-headed, too quick to make enemies out of friends. Somehow just bein' around Mack calmed me down and kept my finger off the trigger many a time. I gave Mack Dunn my gun and he gave me his steadyin' hand. Fair trade, eh, Reverend?'

'Fair trade,' The Reverend agreed. 'And what now for you after we go? The trail again? The posses and sleepless nights and—'

His words were drowned out by Mack's excited shout from the gloom. 'There she is – the *Star of Brazil*!'

All stared out into the bay but were barely able to make out the misty silhouette of a large vessel hove to a mile out by the breakwater. She lay motionless in darkness with furled sails. She could easily have been there some time, as the heavier fog was now beginning to rise before a strengthening breeze.

Mack came trotting back to them. He wore no hat and his face was animated.

'How about that, *amigos*? There she is, large as life and just layin' out there waitin' to take us aboard. And just feel that wind!' He rubbed his palms together and grinned hugehe night. 'Ahh, yessss! A big wind and a big boat and a swift run all the way south—'

He broke off to inhale the sea wind, slapped his barrel chest. 'Folks will sure be surprised when they know I'm gone, Reverend. They'll miss me, don't you reckon?' He laughed boyishly. 'You know, to lots of folks I'm a hero. Can you understand that? Me?'

'In time every hero becomes a bore, Mack,' replied The Reverend, in somber mood now.

Mack squinted across at him. 'Guess that's so. You make that up yourself, Reverend?'

'No. A man named Emerson was responsible.'

'Every hero becomes a bore,' Mack repeated sagely. 'Uh-huh, sure do like that one. Harrumph! Where in Hades is that Jack Dollar ? A man'll start chewin' his shell belt if he don't show soon.'

It was silent for a time before someone said, 'Someone comin' now. Must be Dollar.'

Durling gave a soft whistle of a horned lark and the approaching figure halted, his whistle coming back clear and true.

'Danged if he ain't finally learned to do that,' Mack chuckled. 'Does it good too.'

Durling frowned at the approaching figure. 'Too good, seems to me. . . .' The oncoming man dipped from sight in a hollow and when he reappeared was much closer. 'Damn! That ain't Dollar!'

It was impressive to see just how fast Durling and The Reverend filled their hands and Mack leaned

153

forward tensely. Suddenly he gave a whoop and hollered, 'Darry boy!' and threw his arms wide. 'Damnitall, what are you doin' here? Didn't I warn you to keep away . . . I figgered we'd lost you!'

'I figured that's what you were about when you dumped me . . . you were thinkin' of me, like always. But I had to find you and when I spotted Durling heading back this way, I just tagged along.'

He paused, cutting a hard glance at Durling standing silhouetted against the water. 'I want you to know I appreciate your lookin' out for me—' He broke off, forcing a grin. 'But I really had to find out about about you and this fool trip. Don't you reckon it's time you leveled with us?'

'About what?' Old Mack was sober now.

'You know. Back north with you ridin' all over to check your mail . . . your gettin' all excited that last time.' Darien's gesture encompassed their surroundings. 'All this takin' ship south, and all. Don't you reckon we should know what—?'

'I was aimin' to tell you,' Mack cut in, turning to glance at the ship now hove to behind him. He spread his hands. 'You see, boys, there's a lady. Guess I loved her a long time before she got sick of my wild ways and took ship to South America years ago. I didn't care . . . then. I was too crazy and footloose and . . . well, what does that matter now. But recent I realized I was gettin' old . . . realized I needed to settle down with a good woman, and I

154

thought of her. I wrote tellin' her how I felt and asked about her feelin's. That was the letter I was hopin' for as we came south . . . and finally it came. . . .'

He paused and spread his hands. 'OK, you gotta know. I'm takin' ship for Brazil in an hour . . . and I'll miss every ugly one of you for the rest of my life!'

So, did it end there?

It seemed to do so for every man present who'd had the matchless experience of riding with mad and magic Old Mack Dunn, when an hour later he shook the last hand and clambered into the long boat that came in for him from the ship. He immediately turned his back so they wouldn't see his tears and was soon swallowed up by the shimmering colors and lights reflected in the Galveston sea swell set rolling by the big ships in the harbor.

And no man hurt more than Darien Pell. Yet he showed the least emotion of all as he stood apart from the others as Connie Galliard turned away to straggle off towards the city. Only three were left, himself, The Reverend and a brooding E.J. Durling.

'Feeling a touch of sentiment, E.J.?' The Reverend smiled, pausing with the wash of the silvery waves back-dropping his lean form.

'Like hell!' Durling hitched at his gunbelt. 'I still reckon he's all talk, like always. I've got big jobs in mind but I'm aimin' to wait here a spell and see if he don't change his mind and come right back.'

'There's one he won't find here if he does!'

Durling and The Reverend both turned sharply at the voice. They gaped when they saw Darien standing twenty feet distant with feet wide-planted and right hand hovering over gun butt, eyes as cold as sleet fixed upon the heroic figure of E.J. Durling.

The Reverend went white. 'Darrie boy, don't be a fool!'

'Keep back, Reverend,' Darien ordered. 'It's me and him . . . and I've been waitin' for this ever since Kansas. Ever since he turned yellow dog and left my best pard to die. So now it's me and him!'

The Reverend stood his ground for an agonized moment before Durling spoke.

'I should have known you were cookin' somethin' in that hick skull of yours, Kaintuck.' The powerful figure moved forward and made a sweeping gesture with his right hand. 'C'mon, make your play, hill-billy, and you'd better have made your peace. Now!'

E.J. Durling's draw was a thing of split-second speed and grace. Yet ever since that day up in Kansas, every single day, Darien had taken off by himself to school himself for this moment. He

156

knew he was fast, but also knew he would need something beyond his best to survive this moment. He dug into some deep resource within himself that was unique to the moment as his hand ripped the .45 from leather, came out naked and glittering, faster than he had ever drawn before or believed he ever might again.

The squeeze of the trigger, the bucking of the big Colt, the mighty crash of the shot.

Durling's gun was almost at firing level when he was flung back with white-hot death impaling him, his snarl becoming a gagging cry of pain and terror.

'For Slim!' Darien shouted and five more slugs slammed into the big figure as it tumbled backwards over a low railing to be swallowed by the dark bay waters. His unfired six-gun lay upon the grass but there was nothing else to be seen of E.J Durling – man of the gun.

Staggering with sudden exhaustion, Darien lowered himself to a lichened old boulder. Voices were raised but they meant nothing. He stared at the weapon in his hand for long moment before tossing it from him where it lay in the grass with a needle thin pencil of smoke rising from the barrel.

He'd done the impossible yet somehow had known he could do it. Never again, most likely, but then what reason would he ever have to shoot a six-gun now?

A hand fell on his shoulder and he looked up into The Reverend's face.

'I should reprove you, Darien, but somehow I can't find it in my heart—' The tall man broke off at the sound of voices. 'Get up, son. Get up and get gone and don't you durst look back until you have Kentucky bluegrass under your boots. And promise me you'll never leave that place or that little girl again, not ever!'

Darien rose and walked away along the levee, dazed and yet elated by what he'd done. He had no gun now and his stride was long and loose. There was a mist before his eyes as he paused by an anchored vessel to glimpse the ship far out there upon moon-silvered waters. He inhaled deeply, thinking of home and of Old Mack, picturing his bobbing rowboat now closing in on that big windjammer . . . wondering if Mack had heard that roar of his gun and was puzzled by what it might mean.

The Texas night wind chopped the water into waves now. With a wind like that in back of him, Old Mack would be a hundred miles south come daybreak.

He rode from town an hour later, a lone figure astride a sound horse. His salute to Galveston as it fell behind was for them all, every man, good or bad who'd crossed his path while he'd been on the run. His last wave was for them all – his friend Slim, the men in the gang, the people he'd met in Kansas City and the badmen along the trails who'd tried to bring him down. He bade them all farewell and would remember them every one ... but maybe none as vividly as he would Old Mack Dunn.

Soon the lights of Galveston were gone behind and he set Kentucky squarely between his horse's ears.